REAPING
THE
IMMORTAL

A NOCTURNE FALLS
UNIVERSE STORY

PAMELA LABUD

REAPING THE IMMORTAL

A NOCTURNE FALLS UNIVERSE STORY

Published by Pamela LaBud

Copyright © 2017 byPamela LaBud

Printed in the USA.

Interior Format

© KILLION
THE
GROUP INC.

Dear Reader,

NOCTURNE FALLS has become a magical place for so many people, myself included. Over and over I've heard from you that it's a town you'd love to visit and even live in! I can tell you that writing the books is just as much fun for me.

With your enthusiasm for the series in mind – and your many requests for more books – the Nocturne Falls Universe was born. It's a project near and dear to my heart, and one I am very excited about. I hope these new, guest-authored books will entertain and delight you. And best of all, I hope they allow you to discover some great new authors! (And if you like this book, be sure to check out the rest of the Nocturne Falls Universe offerings.)

For more information about the Nocturne Falls Universe, visit www.kristenpainter.com/sugar-skull-books/

In the meantime, happy reading!

Kristen Painter

CHAPTER ONE

"WHAT DO YOU MEAN, I don't have a room?" Holly Dent, member of the Fifth Guild of Reapers, stood in front of the registration desk of the Nocturne Falls Woodwynds Inn. Wearing her full Reaper regalia of a black hooded robe and sensible shoes, clutching her ceremonial death scythe in one hand. Her familiar, Artemis — a snow white cockatiel shifter — and her bird cage in the other, Holly knew she must have been a frightening sight.

The only things she wanted was a hot meal and a soft bed. By the looks of it, that wouldn't be forthcoming for quite a while.

The cockatiel hissed in echoed frustration.

It had been a long, cross country train ride. Though they'd had a sleeping compartment, it had been narrow, the mattress hard, and it all reeked of mildew. Oh, yeah, only the best for government workers, right?

"I'm sorry, ma'am. I just don't see your reservation," the desk clerk, a short, wispy-haired wood sprite said. Perched on the top of a two-step ladder, he squinted down at the computer screen.

"That's not possible. The Guild always makes the arrangements."

"And we know they never make mistakes," Artemis

grumbled beside her. "Except for that time in Albuquerque, or again in Lincoln, or Chicago..."

"Bird, please," Holly hissed. She turned her attention back to the desk clerk. "It's all here. My name is Holly Dent and I've got a room reserved through next week, though hopefully, I won't be here more than a few days," she said. "I'm a Reaper, sent by the High Council. You can see that my documents are in order." She reached into her pocket and pulled out the glowing stone.

"Hmm," he said. "I believe there is an error here."

"An error? What kind of error?"

Didn't anybody tell this guy not to mention such things in front of a Reaper? Holly's frustrations manifested in dark clouds that had started to gather overhead. Her mood affecting the weather was just a side benefit. It added to the air of mystique that helped her when dealing with the public.

"It appears that your council's secretary tried to book the room and we informed them that because of annual Black and Orange Ball, we're full and will be booked solid for the next forty-three years."

"You're kidding me."

"It's a very popular holiday around here. Perhaps you could try again in a decade or so?"

Holly leaned closer, standing to her full five-foot-five-inch height.

"Listen to me, you little gremlin..."

"Wood sprite," he said, leaning forward so that they were nearly nose to nose.

"Whatever. The High Council sent me here and here I will be staying. So, you better find me a room." Thunder rumbled around them.

"Okay. What will it be? Vampire, werewolf, gargoyle, witch, warlock, demon, Shinigami, or any number of assorted deities..."

"What are you talking about."

"Just checking to see which one you'd prefer bunking with, because if you plan to stay here, you're going to be sharing a bed. Oh, and I'd watch out for the Shinigami, I hear they tend to bite."

"Great. I get it. There's no room. What am I supposed to do now?"

"Beats me, Reaper. Every Inn, hotel, hostel, motor lodge and kennel is full up. Like I said. Very popular holiday."

Furious, Holly crossed her arms and tapped her foot, trying to figure out where she was going to go for the night. "What about the nearest town? Anything reasonably close?"

"The entire region is filled. You can always try knocking on doors."

"And scare half the town into an early grave?" She motioned to her attire. "The Council can barely keep up with the incoming expirations as it is."

He shrugged. "There's the old Hyland place."

A tiny, almost molecular ray of hope seeped into her soul. "Do they take visitors?"

"You could say that," he chuckled. "It's a funeral home. Got all sorts of space. It's six blocks south on the right. Big scary house. You can't miss it." He handed her back her documentation. "Maximillian Hyland is the Funeral Director. Tell him Woody sent you."

Holly stared at him open mouthed for a few seconds.

"What?" He drew back.

"Woody, the wood sprite? Really?"

He let out an indignant huff. "Is it my fault my parents had a sense of humor?"

He waved her off and then popped out in a cloud of smoke.

The bird in her cage coughed dramatically. "Don't you hate smokers?"

Holly let out a breath. "I'm not very fond of that one."

With that, she turned and walked back down the road, dragging her luggage behind her. "Easy does it, big foot," Artie squawked at her. "You're getting seed everywhere."

"Be quiet, bird, or I'll take you to the nearest cat rescue."

"Not funny, Reaper girl. So not funny."

It wasn't a long walk, but to Holly, it seemed like miles. Not only that, but the sun was going down and the crispness to the air deepened to a definite chill. Usually, she enjoyed the outdoors, but being so bone tired, suffering from the train's boxed food menu, and downright ticked off, she was not having a good time.

"There it is," Artie said.

"Thanks, Sherlock," she snapped back. Of course, then she felt guilty at talking to her best friend that way. "Sorry."

"You're a hot mess right now. Think nothing of it."

Wow, she thought as she arrived at her destination. The funeral home, looked like a stereotypical funeral home — right out of the eighteenth century. "Do you think the place has running water?"

"Hey boss," the bird said as it preened its chest feathers. "That name sounds familiar."

Ready to fall over, Holly dragged herself up the last few yards to the front door, setting down Artie's cage and pulling out her cell phone. A few clicks and she was on the app with her assignment listing.

That's when it hit her. "Oh, man," she sat on the railing. "It can't be possible."

"What?"

"It's our guy. Our subject. Maximillian Hyland is the client I'm supposed to Reap."

"Huh. How about that," the bird said. "Well, this might

be the shortest Reap in all of history. If we hurry, we can be on the next train out of here."

Before Holly could answer, she heard a creaking sound and looked up to see the funeral home's front door opening.

Jumping to her feet and wishing she'd had the chance to freshen up before dispensing her duties, she looked up to stare in the face of her next job.

And stopped dead in her mental tracks.

This guy wasn't just drop-dead gorgeous. He was stunning. Warm brown eyes found her first, followed by a square jaw and dimples that took her breath away. And, to top it all, his chestnut hair was long enough to touch the top of his shoulders.

Her heart nearly jumped out of her chest, which would have been a bad thing for anybody, let alone a Reaper.

And, then there was the rest of him. Slender, but muscular, with a swimmer's body, dressed in an Armani suit, exquisitely filling out every inch of the fabric.

"Hi," she finally managed to say in a voice that sounded like the cross between a frog's croak and a strangled cat.

"Well, hello." He glanced around her to see her rolling suitcase, back pack, and bird cage. "Come to arrange a funeral service, have we?"

Dear god. He had a British accent.

For the next few seconds, Holly's emotions went from completely gaga to *holy crap*. She was a Reaper. He was her Reap-ee. Immortal or not, he was going to be crossing into the next ethereal realm and she was going to the next job. A nursing home in Omaha, if she remembered right.

Worse yet, Reapers had a sworn code to follow. She had to tell him the truth at the moment of their meeting.

"Hi, again. I was sent here by Woody, and he said that

since every place in town was full that you might have a room I could rent for a while. Oh, and one more thing..."

"What's that?"

She reached into her pouch and pulled out the affidavit. "I'm Holly Dent, officer of the Fifth Guild of Reapers and by the order of the High Council...I've come for you."

Max couldn't believe his eyes. A small framed woman dressed in a black robe that only hinted at the slender but curvy figure beneath, stood staring wide-eyed at him, a three-piece luggage set and a decorative bird cage sitting on the porch beside her.

Stunning was the first word that came to his mind. A riot of thick auburn hair that she'd unsuccessfully tried to control in the hood of her robe, framed her heart-shaped face. Almost immediately, her clear emerald eyes captured his attention and held him in thrall. Add to that a flawless porcelain complexion with a smattering of freckles across her nose and she was beyond attractive. Hers was a beauty that captured one's soul.

While she might have been mistaken for a Wandering Waif, or Woodland Fae, he instantly sensed she was not. A strong magic emanated from her. And, judging by the clouds stirring in the sky above them, she could be dangerous.

Deep within him alarm bells rang but he was never one to back away from danger.

Especially when it was contained in such an amazing package.

"I beg your pardon?"

She huffed, obviously frustrated. Clearing her throat,

she tilted her head to stare up at him.

"I said, I'm from the Reapers Guild and your number has come up. You're about to take the long trip on the Styx, you know, the boat ride to the afterlive, enter into an ephemeral existence..."

"They still do that? Um, the boat and all?"

She ground her jaw and Max swore her eyes grew a shade darker. "It's a figure of speech. Bottom line, you surrender your soul and I do the rest." She stepped forward and held her hand out to him.

Max took a step back and put his hands up. "Right. Um, well, I'm afraid you've been mis-informed. Some sort of cock-up here at the front office, I imagine. I'm an Immortal."

"Immortal, tinker, tailor, spy, whatever, I've been given orders to Reap you".

Max crossed his arms and considered her a moment.

"I'm not going," he said at last.

Her green eyes grew wide. "Seriously? You think you can refuse?"

"Did you not hear me say immortal? As in, not going to die? Ineligible for death? Beyond the reach of mortality?" He started to close the door.

She lunged forward. "Wait!"

The commanding tone of her voice stunned him. His better senses told him to turn away, run inside, lock the door, and not come out for a century or two.

Max stayed rooted to the spot. When a very attractive woman stood on your front porch, demanding your attention, you didn't simply turn away. Even if she meant to take your life.

"Yes?"

"I need a place to stay. I came a very long way to get you and the hotel where I was supposed to stay got overbooked. Woody said that sometimes you open up your home." She stopped and looked at the 'Funeral Home' sign with a shudder. "For tourists."

There was no way he was going to let her 'Reap' him. If he were anything but immortal, he would have no say about it.

Under the law, most magical beings had to accept their fate when claimed by a Reaper. Of course, some were either very long lived or immortal. Some followed the path to the hereafter on their own, others were subject to soul collectors like Holly.

It was confusing enough as it was. But, he'd heard the Guild had been pushing for more legislation recently. Was claiming Immortals part of those changes?

Unfortunately, Max was not the best on keeping up with current events. Especially since 'current' to Max meant within the last five-hundred years or so.

Immortals were beings that existed outside of time. They could pick and choose how they walked through eternity.

So, no matter what orders she'd been given, Max doubted she was any real threat.

"You can stay, but this is a funeral home and therefore a no Reaping zone. What do you say?"

He meant to say more but almost immediately sensed immense power inside her. Her emotion was demonstrated by the wind rising around them. He suspected that if she chose to, she possessed enough power to take out a city block.

"It's not like I have a lot of choice, now do I?"

Max knew it wasn't in his best interest to give in to sarcasm, but he couldn't help himself. Something in her serious expression made him want to tweak her temper just a bit.

Grinning, he bowed formally. "You're welcome. Please, come in."

He held the door and she stomped by him, clearly not happy about the arrangement. "I don't require much," she told him. "A clean bed, an early wakeup call and a continental breakfast will be fine."

Max chuckled.

"Your room is on the second floor, first door on your right," he called after her. To his surprise, she'd left her baggage in the door way. "Oh, here, let me help you with your luggage."

Not waiting for her to comment, he lugged her suitcases up the stairs.

"Hey! You forgot me."

Max spun around when he remembered there was yet one more guest staying with her. The small, rounded birdcage. Leaving the luggage at the top of the stairs, he went back and retrieved the animal.

Bending down, he picked up the cage, and lifted the cover to peek inside.

"Well, hello."

It was an albino cockatiel with bright red eyes that glared. The exotic animal leaned forward. "Hello to you."

"Oh, a chatty little fellow."

"Pfft. I'm a lady and I'll thank you to lower my cover. This place has a draft."

"Right." He started to comply and then peered back once again. "You're the Reaper's familiar, right?"

"Well, aren't we a nosy one? I'm more than a familiar. I'm a witch and can turn you to stone if I choose to. So, you'd better watch out, mister."

"Right. A witch that encases itself in feathers, lives in a cage and has no bowel control."

The bird flapped its wings and hissed at him.

Deciding that he'd ruffled the thing's feathers quite enough, Max lowered the cover. The creature was almost as prickly as it's master.

This was one more complication added to a day of them. "A rat with wings."

"I heard that." The bird hissed again.

"Maybe it's time for me to get a cat."

When he'd reached the guest room, he knocked on the door. "Room service." He'd meant it as sarcasm, but somehow, he thought it might be lost on the snappy vixen.

It wasn't the first time he'd taken on guests, and to be honest, he usually enjoyed it. Being an Immortal, he wasn't one to have a lot of friends. Add mortician to that, and well, humans and Magics alike pretty much steered clear of him. Not that he'd hadn't been nice, or even friendly.

Nobody liked to hang around with a guy who dealt with the dead. Heck, even the zombies made it a point to leave his immediate vicinity whenever he entered a room.

As if he'd bother with the *already* dead.

You sucked if the zombies deserted you. They didn't have high standards when it came to friends.

"Thank you," she said, opening the door. "Oh, let me get my wallet."

She'd already removed her robe and Max was delighted to see that despite the austere wardrobe required for her work, she had a fun, quirky side. Wearing a light green, tea length, floral print peasant dress, she accented the scoop neckline with a vintage string of pearls that matched her earrings and bracelet. It was a vintage nineteen-fifties look that ensnared him.

A guy could fall for a woman like her.

Any guy other than Max, that was. He was not a man to fall easy, or even fall at all. As a much younger Immortal, he'd found the girl of his dreams.

Or, he thought he had, but the feelings hadn't been mutual. A young witch who was mortified by having to spend an eternity with one fellow.

Turned out, it was hard to keep the magic alive when one had unlimited time and a heart for roaming. He'd wanted to stay with her for eternity. She ended the relationship after six months. It was a lesson he'd learned the hard way.

But Jessie was ancient history and even though centuries had passed, and he still ran into her from time to time, there was a pang of regret whenever he dredged up those old feelings.

He was so deep in his thoughts that he almost missed the Reaper's next gesture. Looking down he saw that she held out a ten-dollar bill.

"A tip?"

"It's as good as I give, so you better take it."

Max laughed. "I don't take tips, madam. I allow guests here for my friends on the hospitality council, so it's not necessary. And, as for breakfast, I'm not what you'd call an early riser myself, so I suggest you set the alarm clock at the bedside and you may have free range of the house, including the kitchen."

"Oh?"

"Again, this is my home, not a hotel."

"Right. Well then, is there anything else?"

He stood there, mouth open. Was there?

For the first time in ages, he was intrigued. "I suppose not. Um, I've just called for a pizza, if you're interested."

"No thanks. I'm too tired to eat right now. I just need a shower and that bed over there..."

"Good night." He pulled the door shut and stood staring at it for a moment. "What the devil is wrong with me?"

Of course, he had to be careful what he said, because with all sorts of beings around, someone was liable to answer him.

More than his alarming attraction to the Reaper, there was his concern over being Reaped. While he'd like to spend more time with his hot little house guest, he had to be careful. It wouldn't be the first time an Immortal threw away his fate at the hands of l'amour.

That would be bad.

Very bad.

CHAPTER TWO

TO HER DELIGHT, AND FOR the first time in months, Holly slept without a problem. Straight through the night until morning. She would have kept on sleeping, too, if Artemis hadn't started her early morning birdsong.

"Really?" She cracked one eye open and peered at the white cockatiel.

"What?" the bird squawked.

Flopping back in the bed, Holly bit down a curse. "You're not singing, are you? And since when do Cockatiels like Pavarotti?"

"Hey." The bird rustled its feathers. "For your information, I've had classical training."

"Really?" Holly sent her friend a sideways look.

The bird huffed and turned its tail feathers upward. Of course, Holly knew that Artemis wasn't strictly of the avian persuasion. But, she was not an opera singer, either.

Not wanting to pluck her friend any further, Holly turned on her side and pulled the blanket up over her head. Not at all like your standard hotel bed, the guest bedroom in the funeral home was quite comfortable. and not nearly as off-putting as it looked from the street.

Though an unusual lodging, the place had old style charm to it. From the comfy feather bed, to the lace curtains on the windows and the polished hardwood floor, it was beyond nice.

The place was charming.

Of course, if you had a bent for such things, that was great. Holly, not so much. She preferred a more urban setting, and while she was long overdue for a vacation, this was definitely not her ideal getaway.

She had to admit, the Nocturne Falls brochures were inviting, and like every other person of the magical persuasion, she'd once considered settling down here when her Reaper bid was over. Now that she was here, trapped in small town goodness, she realized it probably wasn't for her.

She liked deep sea fishing or dense South American trails. But snoozing in a quaint village?

Not her cup of tea.

"Mmm, tea."

A gentle tapping sounded on her bedroom door.

"Hello?" A young woman's voice called from the hall. "Miss Dent? I've come to tell you that breakfast is ready. Mr. Max doesn't keep the spread out long, so you better get down there."

"He said he didn't do breakfast for his guests?"

"Oh, he doesn't. In fact, you're the first. It's a bit of a surprise, actually."

Who's he trying to impress? Well, she didn't need special favors, that was for sure.

Holly sat up and stretched. "I don't suppose there's a donut shop anywhere nearby?"

"Uh, not close, no."

"Right. I'll be down in ten." Of course, he'd intimated that she'd be doing her own cooking. Well, it looked like maybe he wasn't too enthused about having guests but he knew that they would have to eat.

Holly's stomach growled.

The woman giggled. "Um, better make it seven."

Before Holly could argue further, the footsteps disappeared within seconds. "A witch. He's an Immortal who employs a witch."

Artemis squawked behind her. "How do you know she's his servant? Maybe she's his girlfriend. Or, wife..."

Holly didn't know why, but the thought of the tall, handsome funeral Director-Immortal being in a relationship with a cute witch didn't sit well with her.

Holly's only concern was that she faced as little opposition as possible when she Reaped the guy. After all, a screaming, hysterical loved one made it unpleasant for everyone. It's not like they couldn't get together in the afterlife.

Few people even considered that. Still, even for the romantic, living had a term limit. Death was forever.

Holly rubbed her eyes. "I'd better get on with it," she told Artemis. "This guy's not going to Reap himself. Of course, I suppose I could have a muffin and a cup of coffee before I get to work, right?

Busy munching on a fresh honey and seed stick, Artemis had little to say. It was clear that she didn't like being interrupted during her meal. When Holly flicked the cage, she was rewarded with the bird version of a spitting, wing-fluttering hissy fit.

"Whatever," the bird squawked.

Twenty minutes later, Holly was dressed in her 'time to get serious' outfit which consisted of a sensible black pantsuit, pearl jewelry, and her hair pulled severely back into a bun. Nearsighted, she usually wore her contacts, but the long journey and the threat of allergies had made her decide to wear her glasses. She looked like a high school junior wearing grownup clothes, but Holly didn't care.

Slipping on her Reaper robe, she pulled the hood up and took one last look in the mirror.

While she had no bags under her eyes, Holly looked tired. Not the sort of exhaustion that plagued a person after months of traveling — she would have expected that. She noticed there was a slight change in her pallor. There was also a world-weary shadow around her eyes and unmistakable sadness at the set of her mouth. In fact, to anyone who knew her, she was sure she looked down-right depressed.

And Depression never looked good on a Reaper.

"It'll have to do," she told her reflection.

The minute she opened her bedroom door, she smelled the thick scent of fresh baked cinnamon rolls and hot coffee. It was just like that sweets place at the mall when she was a kid.

Making her way to the first floor, Holly followed the smell of cinnamon until she reached the dining table.

"Hello," the proprietor said. He stood and motioned to a chair at the table. "Let Millie set you up. Coffee? Juice? Water?"

Almost giddy from the smell of food, Holly could barely answer. "All three, please. And one of those lovely buns."

"Of course."

Suddenly, a woman appeared from out of nowhere. Short, round and wearing a cheerful expression, she looked like a typical British maid, complete with black dress, white cap and apron.

"Hullo, Miss. Good morning to you."

Before Holly had a chance to thank her, the servant set a plate complete with cinnamon bun and fresh cream cheese icing in front of her. A hot cup of coffee and a small juice glass followed in short order.

"Oh my," Holly said, giving the woman a sideways

glance. "This looks amazing. How did you know..."

Her host cleared his throat. "Millie is an ephemeral, you know, a ghost with psychic abilities."

"I know what an ephemeral is."

"Right. Anyways, since she knows what I want before I do, I find her a great time saver."

"Oh, wow." Holly looked at the plate before her. "That looks fantastic."

"Wait until you taste it. Positively orgasmic."

That was when it happened. The man's voice definitely had an effect on her. Suddenly, she had a flash of herself engaging in a deep, sensual kiss with her host.

Holly shook her head. "Oh, um. Okay."

She picked up her fork and cut off a nice chunk of the cinnamon bun and popped it into her mouth. Her appetite flared and before she knew it, she'd eaten the bun, finished her second cup of coffee and downed the juice in a single swallow.

Her host, on the other hand, hadn't even touched his own meal.

"You do have a healthy appetite."

Refusing to feel embarrassed, Holly quickly wiped her mouth. "That was amazing. I didn't eat lunch yesterday and dinner on the train..."

"Was less than adequate. I completely understand. It's one of the reasons I abhor travel. Of any kind."

Holly sat back, finally sated, and at the same time glad that there wasn't more food on the table to tempt her. "It must be a very sad life you lead, staying at home all the time. Dealing with death at every turn." A thought occurred to her. "I can relieve those feelings of loneliness and boredom. I can help..."

Leaning forward, she gazed deep into his eyes, drawing him in and using all the persuasive powers her position as a soul collector had gifted her with.

"Really?"

"Think about it. No more pain and suffering. Only peace."

To her delight, her subject stared back at her, obviously caught in her spell, pulled toward her by the tone and timbre of her voice. In the space of a few short breaths, he would surrender to her and once her control was locked onto him, they'd begin their journey to the after world. It saddened her a little, though. He'd fallen so easily. In truth, she would have welcomed a challenge.

"I promise," she told him.

Then, in the next second, her control bubble popped and he burst into laughter. Loud, obnoxious, and absurdly adorable. If she hadn't been so angered at his ruse, she might have enjoyed his laughter.

"You thought you had me, didn't you?" He howled, slapping the table as he laughed. "I don't know when I've been so amused. You were such an easy target."

"Right." Acting way more ticked off than she was, Holly crossed her arms and sat back in her chair. "Joke all you want, laughing boy, this is serious. The order is here. You must come with me. It's the law."

He settled down and though she was sure it was more for her benefit than for decorum, he swallowed back his mirth and sent her a more serious expression.

"So, I've heard. But, it's not my law."

"You're a member of the race of Magics, aren't you?"

He shrugged. "That's where it gets a bit twisty. Actually, I'm not. Because of my immortal status, I'm not considered human. Other than living a long time, I don't have any magical power. I don't sustain myself off blood and have no advanced powers of sight or speed. Nor do I shift to a different form or wield spells. I'm just your run of the mill..."

"Immortal," she finished for him. "Whether you believe it or not, not dying is a sort of magic. The papers I have..."

"Are wrong. Now, you're welcome to stay at my home if you like, but this Reaper nonsense will not be tolerated."

He stood up and threw his napkin on the table, grinning as if he were the cat who'd just consumed all the cream.

Holly ground her jaw. Maximillian Hyland might as well have slapped her with a glove. It was a challenge and she'd never been one to run off with her tail between her legs.

"Fine." She stood up, matching her stance to his. "You should know, I'm going to be here as long as it takes."

"Well then, I hope you can figure it out by the end of the week. Then, the festival is over and, room or no room, you're outta here."

"You're going to throw me into the street?"

He'd reached the door, not even turning around as he yelled back. "Watch me."

And watch him, she did.

As he turned and walked out of the room...

Of course, it wasn't a bad view. The guy was drop dead gorgeous. Broad shoulders, narrow waist, long, lean limbs and a swagger that could make a girl swoon. Dark brown hair and hypnotic silver eyes, with a British accent, too.

He'd been made to drive women wild.

"I'm not just any woman," she muttered under her breath. And, though she'd met some pretty attractive people in her time as a Reaper, she'd never considered dating one.

But, she thought, if she were to ever fall for any of her clients, this guy would be the one.

Shaken by the power behind that thought, Holly knew

that she could no longer trust herself.

"It's time to call in the big guns," she muttered, rising from the table. Pulling out her cell phone, she started to ask where she could make a private call, Millie appeared in front of her.

"The den is down the hall, on the right, Miss. Very private."

"Right." She needed to get this Reap done. Having someone serve your every whim could get addictive. Not to mention, distracting.

"Don't get used to it," she muttered to herself.

Besides, Mr. Hyland was certainly distracting enough on his own.

While Max had made a grand exit from the dining room, he hadn't felt as confident about his future as he'd let on. Thanks to a late-night internet search, he'd learned that more and more Immortals were being hit with 'living beyond estimable time' litigation. Basically, the High Council of Reapers was looking at the length of life issues and how it affected those of the 'less' long-lived races. Though none had been successful to date, it was a very real possibility that the same circumstances which had made Immortals safe from Reapers, was now the very thing that might be their undoing.

Something had to be done and fast.

Unfortunately, that meant he'd have to take some drastic measures. First of which involved calling on the last person on the planet he wanted to deal with.

"Yes, I've been trying to reach Matthew Highland for twenty minutes. I know he's there. Tell him I need to speak with him and it's not about the money he owes me." He waited, tapping his foot impatiently.

Matthew, or rather Matty as he was called by everyone

who knew him, was not good with handling money. A few decades back, he'd been in a bit of a financial strait and, against his better judgment, Max had helped him out.

If that were they only issue between them, Max would have let it go. But, the truth was they hadn't been close for a few decades. Words had been said in haste and all. Deeper things were left unresolved between them. Now, more than ever, they needed to stand united. If he had to plead a case in front of the High Council, it would be better for them to stand together.

The night before, when he'd taken the cute little Reaper in and given her shelter, he'd thought he was simply being a good Samaritan. He thought that all her ramblings about him being her next Reap was a result of late night confusion, public drunkenness, or an unbalanced mind. Perhaps all three.

But then, when he'd sat with her at the breakfast table, he realized how serious she was, and, combined with his research, a real threat hovered over him.

Which was too bad because, even with her intention of ending is life, she was the most fascinating person he'd ever met and it took all his resolve to keep his distance.

All his resolve.

Thankfully, Max's thoughts on his guest were cut short when his brother finally answered his call.

"Hello, Max, my bro. How goes it?"

"Why is it whenever you need money, I'm on your speed dial and when there's even a hint I might need something, you suddenly disappear?"

"Maxie. You don't think I avoid you on purpose? That I only reach out for you when I need something and then the rest of the time pretend you don't exist?"

Of course, that's exactly what Max thought, but it would do no good to push the point. And, to be fair, he did want something.

"I hate to bother you, but I need some info. Someone has mixed up files and I've got a Reaper on my hands who has a contract on me."

"You? Are you sure? Like, we're immortal..."

"I know..."

"Supposed to live forever..."

"I know that, too." Max did his best to stay patient with his twin.

"Did you tell her that?"

"I did. She's most insistent."

The truth was, his younger-by-ten-minutes twin brother was into a lot of things. Bad things. Like organized crime and under official radar things. For their entire adult life, Max had managed to avoid learning too much about Matty's life, but on occasion, he had proved useful.

Max was the straight arrow and his twin was a little bit fluid when it came to going around corners. While he would have preferred to keep his distance, it looked like Max was going to have more than a few corners ahead of him now.

"A determined woman. Don't you hate when that happens? I haven't heard anything. Then again, I haven't exactly had my ear to the magical turf, if you get my meaning. Give me a few days and I'll get back to you."

"Thanks, and hey, no longer than that, eh? This chick is determined to take me, no matter what. If she calls in the big guns, we may end up attending a funeral."

"No kidding. Where you goest, I goest," Matty said. His somber tone was not a joke. Twin Immortals — only alive if the other lived. In their case, it was a two for one ride on the river of life.

"Right. Talk to ya, soon."

Max set his phone on the table and sat back in his chair.

While he didn't want to accept that he'd been called to pay the ferryman, it was a distinct possibility.

Just then a gentle tapping sounded at his study door. "Yes?"

His secretary, Melody Tanner stuck her head in the room. A classic brunette beauty, she bore a resemblance to a young Liz Taylor, violet eyes and all. A vibrant witch, she could have spent her days spinning one spell after another. Why she chose to work in a funeral home was beyond him. Not one to question his good luck, he'd been glad to hire her and decided that her choice of career was just that — her choice, her business.

"Beg pardon, Mr. Hyland, but there is a Mr. Egalton Grayson here to see you. He says he wants to discuss his final arrangements."

"Grandfather Grayson? Are you serious? That old warlock is probably going to outlive me."

His secretary chuckled. "Oh, he knows that, sir. He said he just wants to be prepared."

"Wants to help himself to my liquor cabinet, more like it." Max looked at his now darkened cell phone, willing it to ring. He knew he wasn't going to be that lucky. "Tell him I'll be right there."

"Yes, sir." Molly closed the door and once again Max was alone. All he could think of was his predicament and the lovely little Reaper in his den. Surely, she was up to no good. If only he had a familiar to send up there to spy on her.

He could ask Millie, but the ephemeral couldn't be depended on to work in his favor. More than likely, she'd end up helping the wayward visitor and unwittingly get him a closer to his own demise.

That was the thing about ephemerals. They didn't make good spies.

Max scoffed. He wasn't one for invading anyone's privacy. He knocked that thought down right away. "I'll find a way out of this, and it won't involve being dishonest." He had a code of honor, after all.

Once Grayson left, after eating an entire tray of cookies and downing almost two bottles of his most expensive brandy, Max was finally free for the rest of the afternoon.

Having missed both breakfast and lunch, he was ruminating on how a nice bowl of clam chowder would taste awfully good at that moment, but his attention was grabbed once again by Ms. Dent.

Rounding the corner into the main hall, he couldn't help overhearing his guest chatting on her phone.

"Master Renault, I understand what you're saying, but he is refusing to accede to my authority."

Max crossed his arms and leaned against the wall beside the den's doorway. Ordinarily, he wasn't one to eavesdrop, but since his very existence was at stake, he gave himself permission.

"Yes, sir. I know. I hate to ask this of you, but, you've been my teacher, my mentor and my friend. He's extremely resistive to my magic, and more powerful than even the High Council believed when they assigned me his case. I need your help."

Peering around the door frame, Max saw her standing, as tense as a cable pulled taut. Even though she was trying to end him, he had to admit, she was beautiful. Had he not been concerned about her taking his life, he would have made a play for her.

As it was, he needed to thwart her efforts and send her on her way.

"You will?" she said, her entire body relaxing. "Thank you. I'll be looking forward to your visit."

Hearing her click off the phone, he ducked back in the

hallway. The last thing he needed was for her to discover him spying on her. Just as he slipped out of the hall and into the foyer, he grabbed the mail from the table beside the door.

"Oh, Mr. Hyland," she said, slightly out of breath, her cheeks pink with excitement. "I'm glad I've run into you. I wanted to let you know I've a friend coming. Would you able to accommodate him as well?"

"I'm sure arrangements can be made. When will he arrive?"

"Tomorrow afternoon."

He nodded. "He won't be staying in your room?"

Her pink cheeks reddened. "He's not that sort of friend."

"I see. Do you want him to be?"

It was a cold question and Max knew he shouldn't be so direct, but he couldn't help himself.

"That isn't your business, now is it?"

She was single and for a reason he didn't understand, Max was glad of it. He shrugged and gave her a lopsided grin.

"No, it's not. Sorry. I'm not an experienced innkeeper, you know. The reason I asked was to see if I needed to have another room prepared."

"Oh," she said, clearly more than a little shaken. "My apologies." She cleared her throat. "Master Renault is my mentor. I apprenticed with him for ten years."

"Wow. Ten years? I didn't realize that Reaping was a skill."

To his surprise, her face reddened even more. Clearly, he'd touched a nerve.

"For your information, escorting the soon to be deceased to the afterworld is a delicate and complicated job."

Max stepped back. "I apologize for my ignorance. Tell you what. How about I make it up to you?"

"Make it up to me?"

"Absolutely. There is a quaint little diner within walking distance. It'll be on me."

"I don't know..." She chewed her lip. "Policy doesn't allow Reapers to engage in social interaction with our subjects."

"Oh, come on. This isn't an engagement. Heck, it's not even a date." He could see her wavering. "I assure you, I will be a perfect host. Come on. Reapers eat, right?"

"Of course, we do."

"It's just a meal."

"Right."

"Um, one thing..."

"What?"

She tipped her head sideways which improved her cuteness factor. Cute squared? It boggled his mind.

She started to walk away but Max touched her shoulder. "Your robe. You might want to leave that here."

"I can't. Reapers are only allowed to dress in civvies when they're not working. Now that I'm on a job..."

Max grimaced. "Yeah, but if you go out in that costume, people are going to talk. Once they realize who you are and what you're here for, there will be widespread panic. And, there are lots of tourists here, into the thousands even. Can you risk it?"

"Right." She shook her head. "I've never been in this situation before. And, I'm pretty sure there's no mention of it in the policy and procedure manual."

"So, dinner?"

Max held his breath as she wavered. "Okay. Let me change."

"I'll be in the dining room when you're ready."

With that, she turned and headed toward the stairwell. He'd always had a thing for redheads. Add her quick wit and determined manner, she was literally his dream girl. Luckily, he wasn't the sort to fall for a woman so easily, or he'd be a goner.

"So, whatcha doing, Boss?"

Max whirled around to see Melody behind him, leaning on the doorjamb.

"Nothing," he said, standing straight and doing his best to keep a guilty expression from his face.

"Looks to me like you were checking out that little Reaper lady." She wiggled her eyebrows at him and pushed away from the door. "Come on, boss. You don't have to lie to me."

"As if," he said. "She wants to Reap me, for magic's sake. Besides, you know I don't do that mushy boyfriend-girlfriend stuff."

Melody laughed. "Well, maybe you should."

Before Max could further argue the point, she giggled and in her witchy way, waved a dismissive hand at him and sauntered past.

"You're being ridiculous," he called after her, but she'd already started up the stairwell.

If he was that transparent with his secretary, how long would it be before the Reaper caught on?

He had to get this resolved and soon, or he'd be doomed.

Seriously, end of life doomed.

CHAPTER THREE

THE FIRST THING HOLLY REALIZED was that she'd made a huge mistake.

After spending most of the day trying to connect with her former teacher, she was glad for the chance to take a break. Although she'd been unable to complete her assignment by herself, and the man beside her was the reason, she refused to feel like a failure.

But now, having dinner with the guy she meant to end, she couldn't help feeling like she'd given up too quickly. That she'd let his amazing good looks and clever conversation sway her better judgment.

"Wow, this place is really homey," Holly said as her host ushered her into the restaurant. It was a big, open cabin-style room. There were polished wood tables, a giant hearth in the center of the room, the windows even had homespun curtains. Every table had an old-fashioned oil lamp and woven place settings.

"Told you. And, they have the best food you'll ever taste. I promise."

"Right."

The hostess, a middle aged grandmotherly type wearing a blue checkered dress, a white apron and white waitress shoes, met them at the door. "Howdy, Max. I see you've got company this evening."

"Yes, Mrs. Miller, I do have uh..." He shot a blank expression at Holly.

"Business associate," Holly said, practically pushing herself in front of him. "We know each other through work."

The woman's bright expression dulled a little. "Are you a funeral director, too?"

Oh, gosh, Holly nearly swallowed her tongue. "Um, no..."

"She's with the casket company. Lovely, job they do, too. Did you see Mrs. Branson's case?"

The hostess lost all her color. "Oh my goodness, um, was that your work?"

Holly gave her a weak smile. "Not mine, directly, but um I know the person who made it. At the factory, I mean. He didn't make it on his own..." Of course, she had no idea just how they made the darn things.

Holy cow, she thought. *Did I just lie to a stranger?* What next? Sleeping with him?

He must have sensed her unease, because he stepped forward. "I'm sorry to interrupt, but I'm really starving. Do you have a table open?"

The woman was visibly shaken but nodded. "Of course. Follow me."

Once they were seated, her subject leaned forward. "Are you a vegetarian? Any food allergies I should know about?"

Holly nearly bit her tongue. "Awfully personal, don't you think?"

"Sorry, I should have prefaced my questions first. They have the best prime rib here you'll ever eat or if you like, there's chicken or salmon, both of which they cook in peanut oil..."

She put up her hand. "The prime rib sounds great to me."

"Allow me to order for you."

"Maybe another time," she said before she realized that it gave credence to his intentions of avoiding his Reaping.

Without saying a word, he waved the waitress over and when she came, the statuesque blonde gave Holly a once over, she smiled at Max. "Hey gorgeous, what can I get for you?"

He smiled up at her and for a moment Holly thought the two might be having a thing. *Great*, she thought. *I'm going to be the third wheel on this two-wheeler.*

Before she could comment on it, though, he turned his smile to her and it grew wider.

"Beer or wine?"

She smiled. "Ice tea."

He nodded. "Two iced teas, Miss Heather."

"Right away," the woman said in a breathless tone as she retrieved the menu's.

"Thank you," Holly said, almost pushing her menu at her. "I'll have the Cesar Salad and a plate of spaghetti."

"Ah, no prime rib, then?"

"I think I need to stay away from red meat tonight. Maybe another time."

The Immortal smiled up at the waitress. "Then, I'll have the antipasto and lasagna."

Holly watched as the waitress leaned across the table, showing her ample bosom. A little bit ticked off that the woman had practically thrown herself on her—

Oh, wait, she thought. *He's not my date.* Surprised and a little bit angry for even thinking such a thing, she did her best to reassure herself. It was just a meal and he was her subject. Once she and Master Renault had him under control, this magical being would be safely on his way...

Holly cringed. She was not one to shirk her duties, but this charming, amazingly handsome guy was going to be

Reaped and it kinda bothered her.

Well, it had been awhile since she'd had a guy in her life...

"So," he said, shooting her another amazing grin. "Tell me all about yourself..."

Holly looked at him. "There's not much to tell, Mr. Hyland. I'm no one special." She looked across the room, suddenly uncomfortable under his gaze.

He reached across the table and touched her hand. "I'm sure that's not the truth at all. And, please, call me Max. I'm not one for formality."

He smiled at her and Holly was suddenly aware of just how charming this man could be. "I am, Mr. Hyland," she said, pulling her hand back. "I appreciate your sentiments, but you've no need to placate me. In fact, I think it best, that we keep this on a professional level."

The waitress returned and put their salads in front of them. Holly busied herself with arranging her plate and didn't dare look up at him.

But, he wouldn't let it drop.

"So, I'm to go on calling you Ms. Dent?"

"Reaper Dent," she said. "That is my title, after all."

"Well, it's a bit silly, don't you think? I mean, here we are enjoying a meal and sharing pleasant conversation. It would be like me insisting that you call me Funeral Director Hyland."

Holly shrugged. "I think Director Hyland would be sufficient. Dignified, in fact."

He grinned at her and plucked an olive from the antipasto tray and popped it in his mouth.

"Oh," she said, not realizing that she'd spoken, suddenly entranced by the shape of his mouth and the way his jaw worked as he finished his food.

"Excuse me?"

Suddenly embarrassed, Holly looked down at her food. The last thing the Immortal needed to see was her mooning over him like a love-starved teenager.

"Nothing," she said, clearing her throat. "I was just remembering some paperwork I have to finish."

The waitress appeared with her helper arms laden with their entrees. Two heaping plates, a basket of bread and a pitcher of tea. Holly watched as she filled both the glasses and set the remainder aside.

"Will there be anything else?"

"No, thank you," the Immortal grinned. "I think we can manage for now."

Damn, she thought. This man was smooth. It didn't help that the waitress practically melted right in front of them.

"That was a wonderful meal," Holly said, settling back and wishing she could spend the night just being a girl out with a guy.

Unfortunately, that was impossible.

Unfortunately, that was impossible.

Once you're a Reaper, you're always a Reaper. Except, of course if you could convince the Council that you were ready for retirement. Or, if they deemed you unfit for the job.

Either way, at least for now, Holly would be a Reaper, and the handsome, charming, and very clever Immortal in front of her was her target. She'd have to take his soul, or die trying.

"Is everything okay?" He asked, wearing a darn near swoon-worthy expression of concern.

"No. I think I'm still tired from the trip." Or, that she was a frustrated young woman with no hope of having a normal life.

"So, what made you want to become a Reaper?"

Holly's breath caught in her throat. "Why would you

ask that?" Was he reading her thoughts? Was he one of those mages who also read one's aura or had he done some sort of search online and discovered her entire life?

"Just curious." He sat back. "I think I see where this is going. Look, I know this is an awkward situation. I didn't mean to put you off."

"I know."

Holly looked at him for a moment, and her breath caught in her throat. What was it about this guy? He was her subject and here she was letting him winnow into her heart like a puppy snuggling under a blanket.

"So, how about we make this night complete. I know this absolutely amazing ice cream shop. It will change your mind about desserts forever, I promise." He stood up and held his hand for her. "Are you game?"

"Sure," she said, breathless. Unable to help herself, she rose from her seat and took his hand. "But just this once."

"Gotcha." He nodded.

Holly sensed that convincing him there was no chance for anything to happen between them was not a problem.

But, convincing herself was an entirely different matter.

Like a sugar dependent kid in a big box candy store, Max just couldn't help himself. The Reaper was seriously affecting his judgment. She was sweet and kind, and clearly struggling with her own feelings. It was like she wanted to claim his soul, but found it to be the most detestable act ever.

In other words, seriously conflicted.

Not so different from his own dilemma.

Like, who didn't want to be immortal? No worries about long suffering illness that end in death and despair. No need for 'final' arrangements. And, no saying good-bye.

Well, that wasn't entirely true. Because, unless you secluded yourself to a life only with other Immortals — a place that didn't exist — then you were stuck with the rest of the mortal world. And, everyone else besides you died. You were reminded again and again that every time you said hello, there waited a tragedy in your future for that inevitable and final goodbye.

"How far away is this mind-bending ice cream shop?" she asked, her eyes clouding with a hint of doubt.

"Just a couple of blocks away. After, if we turn right on Rosemont street, we'll be back at the funeral home. A nice stroll for an evening, I think. I've made it many times."

"So, do you usually tempt your lady friends to a fantastic dinner and then follow up by sweetening your approach with ice cream?"

He grinned, though felt a bit shameful at being discovered so easily. "I have been known to frequent this route on occasion."

She laughed. "Since this isn't a date, you're off the hook. But, with your next potential paramour, I'd recommend mixing it up a bit."

"Good advice. I can always choose Indian food, there is a lovely place about five blocks the other direction and a sweet shop not far from that. Thank you."

"You're most welcome." She sent him a smug grin, but it changed abruptly to something darker.

While he wasn't a mind reader, he knew exactly what had crossed her thoughts.

"Ahem," he said. "This conversation turned a bit to the dark side, eh? After all, if you're successful, there won't be any more cozy evening strolls for me. Or, dinners at Aldo's, or ice cream, or, well, anything."

"Sorry. I don't mean to be a downer; it just comes with

the job."

"I'm sure it does."

They arrived at the shop and the moment they entered, the air was filled with the sweet aromas of sugar-laden treats.

"This must be what heaven is like."

Max laughed. "So, let's get down to it. Are you a chocolate girl? Vanilla? Or, the more decadent Neapolitan?"

The woman looked across the expansive counter with the multitude of colorful bins of ice cream. "Um, yes?"

"Of course." He knew instantly what was right for her. "Do you like a little surprise in your ice cream, a sort of sweet, minty mix?"

Her eyes grew big. "How did you know?"

"I'm wise not because I'm so clever, but because I'm old."

"Well then, I bow to your expertise."

Walking to the counter, he winked to the proprietor. "My good woman, my friend and I would like two scoops of your best Spumoni in those tasty sugar cones, please."

"Coming right up." The counter lady, who's name tag read Agnes, grinned.

Ten minutes later they were deeply involved with their treats. Doing his best not to stare, he watched as she daintily lapped at her cone, an expression of euphoria crossed her face, her mouth upturned with joy. His heart flipped when she sat back and her eyes went heavenward.

"You, sir, are a genius," she giggled.

"I'm so glad you think so." And, there were so many more things that he wanted to share with her. His past experiences, for one — the good parts, not the bad. And, of course, he wanted to share his opinions on any number of magically related political issues. He had no care for current events beyond Nocturne Falls. He'd learned long ago not the mix into the affairs of mortals.

"So, would there be a lady Immortal that I should know about?"

He looked up at her, suddenly ripped from his thoughts. "No," he said, surprised at her sudden interest. "The position is available."

Her hand went to her mouth, and she turned a pleasing pink about her cheeks. "I'm not asking for any reason other than to know if there's someone I need contact after..."

There it was again. "No matter how much we try to avoid it, we always come back to the unpleasantness of my mortality."

"I'm sorry. I was trying to learn more about you without being so painfully obvious."

He reached across the table and touched her hand. "You've no reason to apologize. It's your profession, after all."

"Thank you for being so understanding."

"I am curious, though, why get to know your client when you know what you must do?"

She shrugged. "I know it doesn't seem practical, but I think it's important to help a soul transition if you're more understanding of their circumstances."

"For instance?"

She glanced out the window and saw an older couple walking side by side. She had long gray hair pulled in a tight bun and he was nearly bald. The two were deep in conversation — whether about the mundane or more important things, he couldn't tell.

Clearing her throat, she nodded toward them. "I'm guessing they've been together a long time. A half a century, for instance. When one goes before the other, it's a terrible loss. But, it helps for the subject to know that death, like life, is only another level existence. And that, depending on what sort of soul you have cultivated over the years, it's possible to meet up again with their loved ones in the beyond."

"Does that happen much?"

She looked at her hands. "That is the goal," she told him. "Though to be honest, no one knows for sure."

"So, death is as much a mystery to you as it is to every other being, magical or not."

"I'm afraid so."

Quickly pulling her hand back, as if she'd just realized that they were touching, she sent him a sheepish look.

"Then, why do you do it?"

She blinked. "Do what?"

"Reap. Correct me if I'm wrong, but I think it's likely not a thing you enjoy doing."

She sent him a scathing expression. "It isn't a matter of what I like. It's my calling. And, it's a noble profession. Easing one's passing into the next realm is a time honored and necessary pursuit."

"You sound like one of those army recruitment posters."

"It was all I could think of." She put the remainder of her ice cream cone in the cup. "Perhaps we should be heading back."

"Now, it's my turn to apologize. I didn't mean to insult you."

"It's okay," she said, her tone a bit less distressed. "It's only natural to be curious about my job. It's not like you cross paths with a Reaper every day."

He shrugged. "Actually, it's not Reaping that has piqued my curiosity. I've been around many hundreds of years and I'm pretty used to the unsettling nature of mortality, futile and hopeless as it seems. I was more interested in why you chose it?"

"It's a calling," she said, as if repeating the lunch list to a child.

"You said that, but I don't believe it."

"Why not?"

"Because one of the benefits, or curses, depending on how you see it, for living a long life is that I have con-clude there's no such thing as fate but rather it's all about choice."

"Then, you've never been compelled to do something bigger than yourself?"

Well, that was a surprising question, wasn't it?

"I thought so once, but time passed and I realized that I was a fool and mistook what I thought was meant to be as nothing more than a passing fancy. Coincidence rather than fate."

Tilting her head to one side, her mouth formed the perfect little 'o,' and the sight of her expression sent a deep stab into his chest. Dammit all, she was feeling sorry for him.

"Don't do that," he said, suddenly feeling small and unguarded.

"I don't know what you mean?"

"Don't send me that sad-eyed look of sympathy. I'm the lucky one here. I have the gift of immortality and I mean to keep it."

She closed her mouth and pushed back from the table. "I never meant to insult you. Thank you for the dinner and desert. You're most kind."

They stood up and he motioned her to the door and she walked past him in stiff, measured steps. It was clear he'd pricked a nerve and though he knew he would likely regret it later, he felt justified.

"I was just curious," he said once they'd stepped out

into the chilly evening. "Why a person who cares as much as you do would chose such a cold, heartless profession."

She walked ahead of him now, her steps quickening by the moment until he was sure that she would break into a run at any moment. She didn't stop until they reached the corner.

"You know, I find it interesting that you've lived all these years and have never bothered to find out more about the people around you? I only meant to know you better so I could help ease your passing. I've found it beneficial to have a kind hand at a person's back helping them go forward rather than a fist that pushes a person into the abyss."

Her statement felt like a cold slap across his face. He'd been right about one thing, though. She was the most interesting and insightful woman he'd ever met.

And, he was a complete ass.

CHAPTER FOUR

FINALLY, BACK IN HER ROOM, Holly collapsed onto the bed. She hadn't even bothered to undress or even kick off her shoes.

"So, how was your date?" Artemis asked, while she sat on per perch, pecking at the wooden stick beneath her.

"It wasn't a date."

"Really? You, that hot guy, romantic eatery, and — do I scent chocolate? Ice cream, candy, or pie?"

"Ice cream, and again, it wasn't a date."

The bird fluttered her wings and made a sputtering sound. "Call it what you want, you plus hot guy plus four hours together equals date. Do the math, Holly."

"Whatever." Holly yawned. She couldn't remember being this tired — ever. "I'll tell you one thing. He wears me out."

"Hmm, ready for bed and you've not even kissed?" Artemis coughed. "Or, have you?"

"Stop it." Holly rolled over to her side, her back to the bird.

The truth was, a younger, less Reaper Holly would have fallen for this guy in a hot minute. Thankfully, she was no longer that girl. She was grown up, dedicated to her job and to her single life.

That other girl? The one that had spent years waiting

for 'Mr. Right,' had withered into nothingness. There had been no high school sweetheart for Holly. No college boyfriend, no one even remotely interested in her and none that sparked her fire, either. So, she'd gotten the message. And, then the day the Reaper came to call on her grandmother

It'd been a coincidence that she'd been in the room when the old gentleman visited. Tall, lean, and grandfatherly, she'd not expected him to be a Reaper. He'd introduced himself, spoke loving words to her grandmother, and then right before Holly's eyes, she saw the waning light of a soul drift away for the first time.

The stranger told her she had a gift and should consider being a Reaper.

The choice had been clear, and one she'd not doubted until recently when she'd had to Reap a young mother who had a loving husband and three small children.

"Are you still thinking about Mrs. Kelton?" Artemis asked.

Silly bird was always quick to figure her out.

"No. Well, sort of."

"They were prepared for it, you know. She'd been sick a long time."

Holly rubbed her eyes. She would not cry again.

"I know. And, for the record, I'm no longer grieving." The truth was — and her friend knew it — that the very best thing she did for her clients was acknowledge their grief.

Rolling back to her other side, she looked up at the bird. "I just can't help feeling that though their lives are so much shorter than mine and their passing so sad, that they've lived volumes more than me."

"So, you're grieving a life you've never known?"

"Something like that, yes."

The bird cocked its head and ruffled its feathers. "You're thinking about making changes, right? Putting in for your early retirement?"

"I might. I don't know."

"What do you really want?"

Holly looked up at her friend, surprised that she'd never even asked herself that question before. But, the answer popped into her mind immediately.

"Love," she said. "I want to be loved."

"Hello, brother," Matty said, as he pushed the door open. A mirror image to Max, Matty wore a grateful dead t-shirt, faded distressed jeans, and a grin that split from ear to ear.

"What in blazes are you doing here?"

Max was usually a bear in the morning. Without coffee, he was a prehistoric carnivorous beast.

He'd not had coffee yet.

"I know it's an unannounced visit, and I know how much you hate seeing people first thing in the morning, so I brought crullers and coffee."

The previous morning he'd been on his best behavior, drinking a full pot before his breakfast with Ms. Dent. Now, he had no reason to put on airs.

"And you can turn around and take them back. I'm not interested in whatever you have to say."

He started to shut the door, but his annoying sibling stuck his foot in the room and pushed back. "Oh, you'll be interested, brother. I promise."

Max looked at his brother for a long moment.

Looking at Matty these days was like looking at a before digital, old school negative. Max was dark, tanned with mahogany hair and eyes the color of bitter choco-late. Matty had died his hair blond, wore blue contacts and dressed like a wild surfer crossed with a seventies' hair band. Something like, 'California screaming' was how Max saw him.

But, the shape of their faces, the cut of their expressions and the timbre of their voices were the same.

Max had been told that a lot of people felt uncomfortable around them, and he didn't blame them. Where Max was dead serious, Matty was the class clown. Max was organization and Matty was chaos.

And yet, in ways that many people couldn't see, they were very alike. Both were strong willed and stubborn. While they usually stood on opposite sides of an issue, neither one would budge no matter how hard he was pressed.

"Coffee?" Max asked, settling back.

"Whiskey."

Max motioned his brother into his office toward a seat across from his desk. Pulling down a bottle of Scotch, he poured them both a healthy shot.

"So, what is it that has brought you out so early in the day? I didn't think you ever got up before dusk."

To say that his brother preferred the night life was an understatement. More than that, Max was sure his brother's residing in Nocturne Falls was likely the result of something bad. Like a business deal fallen through, or infidelity with one of his associates.

The truth was, Matty preferred urban settings. Vegas, New York City and LA were among his favorite haunts. It must have grated against him to have settled in the quaint little Nocturne Falls.

"I've done some asking around, big brother." He threw back his whisky and smacked the glass on the desktop. "I've heard some, shall we say, unsettling things. Oh, and by the way, it's a good thing you called me. I only found out how much trouble you're in because I've got a connection."

"Connection?"

"Underworld."

A small town about fifty miles away, tucked away from the main roads. It was a gathering spot, rather than a town. A hideaway, really. Not a place decent folks, humans or Magics, frequented. Some said it was no more than a legend, others that it existed in a realm apart from the real world.

That was unsettling enough, but to think of his brother frequenting the place, even worse.

"Really? So, I'm on someone's radar in Underworld? How is that possible?"

Matty shrugged. "Someone's put a contract on you, brother. Who have you ticked off lately?"

"Me? I thought that causing trouble was more your purview than mine. I'm a simple small town businessman."

"Right. Well, somebody not happy with their funeral, maybe?"

Max crossed his arms. "I've had no complaints. But then, undertakers rarely get bad press from their clients since they are dead."

"There are the undead, brother."

"Yeah, well, I don't see too many of them. Or, any of them, in fact." He thought for a moment. "Perhaps I need to put in a call to law enforcement."

"I wouldn't do that," Matty said. "You don't know who you're dealing with. And, can the local cops really help you?"

"Just because this is small town, doesn't mean the sheriff can't do his job. I've seen him. He's a werewolf and he can get really mean."

"Still, take precautions. I know I've not been the best brother, but I rather like being half of a pair. Try not to get yourself whacked, okay?"

Fifteen minutes later, Max stood at the window and watched his brother's little black Porsche pull out of the driveway.

"Everything okay, boss?"

Max turned to see Melody standing at the door. Despite her relatively young age, the witch was no fool. He had a sense she'd been listening in so it'd do no good to lie to her. Besides, having a witch looking out for you wasn't necessarily a bad thing.

"How much did you hear?"

Melody's porcelain completion turned a light pink. "Most of it...well, all of it." She let out a breath. "I'm sorry, Max. I know he's your brother and all, but I don't trust him."

"If it's any comfort, neither do I. But, he showed good faith just stopping by to give me that news in person, so I have to give him credit for that."

"Yeah, credit might be the right word. I suspect it's going to cost you later."

Max sighed. "No doubt." He paused a moment and studied his friend. "Something's bothering you. What is it?"

Melody looked down at her hands and it was clear that something was bothering her.

"I heard through the grapevine that your guest is a Reaper and she's come for you."

"You've been talking to Millie?"

"She's worried about you."

He waved his hand. "It's some sort of mix up. I'm sure we'll get it figured out. I can't be Reaped, you know. The whole 'Immortal' thing."

"Yeah," she said. "I guess you're right. There are laws over this magical stuff."

"Exactly," Max said.

While the analytical side of him knew that was the truth, there was still a niggling of doubt. One thing he'd learned in his long life thus far, was that just because there were laws, didn't mean that could keep them from being broken.

Someone wanted him dead.

Him.

A man without enemies. An Immortal who'd never taken sides in any conflict, Max had no idea why anyone would want him gone. If anything, he'd been a friend to many — the last hundred years or so helping them with their final or faux final arrangements.

So, why put out a hit on him?

And, other than his business, he'd always kept his net worth low. A man of simple means, managing to pay the bills with enough left over to enjoy a few finer things, by no means extravagant. There were plenty of others with more wealth than him.

It wasn't money, then.

After giving Melody a list of things for her to do, supplies to order, appointments to arrange and so on, he returned to his office and retrieved the one record book that no one knew about but him.

'Les Journal,' he'd called it. The one thing that he'd been meticulous about over the years. God help him, but Max was the ultimate record keeper. It was almost a compulsion, really.

Just as he'd opened the tome, a knock sounded at the door.

Hesitating, he thought about putting the book away, but decided against it. Maybe it was time to share it with others. It was so massive, after all, it would take days to go through it. And, by the time he did — and figured out who wanted him dead — it would be too late. So, he needed help.

And, he knew who would be the perfect one to help him.

"Come in," he called out.

The door opened slowly and the very person he was planning to ask for help magically appeared at the door.

"Director Hyland," the Reaper said, poking her head into the room. "I'm sorry to bother you, but I think we need to talk..."

He smiled up at her. "I was about to say the very same thing. Please, come in. Welcome to my sanctuary..."

It was very likely the biggest risk of all, trusting the Reaper.

Destiny on one hand and disaster on the other. What choice did he have?

CHAPTER FIVE

HOLLY WAS NOT USUALLY A person who acted on her impulses. In fact, she was the exact opposite. Forming a plan, examining it for every contingency, and then using every precaution to execute it...

She never jumped into the pool. She went in excruciating inch by excruciating inch. Carefully examining all sides of every issue, calculating and recalculating until she was ready to move forward or run away. And, most of the time, running away was her wheelhouse.

That's one reason why being a Reaper fit so well. She was given orders, performed her job, and moved to the next assignment with little decision making of her own.

So, approaching the Immortal on a whim was so totally out of character for her. She was not that girl. In fact, the fact that she hadn't planned this out to the nth degree scared her to death.

But, she had two very logical reasons for preceding and, next to planning, logic was her god.

First, ever since she'd received her orders, she was sure something was just 'not quite right' about it. She'd Reaped hundreds of people in her short career, mostly humans with a few notable Magics. But, this was different. He was an Immortal — immune to death. Not that these things didn't happen. Long-lived races were Reaped every day.

But, not by her. She was a mid-level operative and the fact that this assignment landed in her lap was more than unusual. It was darn right inconceivable.

The second reason was that try as she might, she just couldn't get him out of her thoughts. Last night had been the worst night she'd ever spent. Tossing and turning, hearing his words, smelling his spiced cologne, and imagining him spending every minute of the day and night beside her. Sharing meals, long walks, late nights and showers...

Before speaking, Holly swallowed a couple of quick breaths. This was getting out of hand and she had never, ever gone for a guy like this. He was a drug and she was the addict. It was downright unsettling.

That was it.

He unsettled her.

"Welcome to my sanctuary," he said, motioning for her to come inside.

"Thank you. I'm sorry to bother you."

He smiled and Holly fairly melted at the sight of it.

"Nonsense. Please, come and have a seat. What do you have in mind?"

For the first time, Holly realized that though she'd had some idea of who this man was, her opinions were based mostly on the external face he'd shown her.

But now, walking into the room that was him, judging by its décor, gave her yet another dimension into the man she'd suddenly become obsessed with.

"Interesting room," she said, not realizing she'd spoken out loud until she heard his laugh.

"Thanks... I think. I know it's a little odd, but I like it."

Odd was an understatement. A wide, expansive space that was dominated by a huge mahogany desk, floor to ceiling windows overlooking what she'd surmised was a 'private' garden, and on the other side of the room, endless rows of bookshelves. Even with her poor understanding of antiques, Holly figured those shelves must have held first print editions of virtually every important book ever written. Beside each bookshelf there were glass cabinets filled with various objects. One, denoted the study of space and the planets judging by the antique telescope, and other instruments designed to measure time and space. On another were what looked like early electronics — phones, phonographs, cameras and televisions from every single period of recent history.

On the final wall, there were amazing works of art — paintings that she couldn't name but were clearly created by the masters.

"Wow," was all she managed to say.

"I know." He motioned her to have a seat at his desk. "I'm sort of a collector."

Holly didn't realize her mouth was open until she had to close it to speak. "I think that's an understatement."

"Lovely to look at, but none of its worth very much, I'm afraid. Well, except for me."

"Are you kidding, those paintings alone..."

"Are mine. I went through an artistic period."

"Really? Because that looks like Monet and that one a Van Gogh..."

He laughed. "Let me clarify. I'm a great 'copier.' Trust me, a true expert could tell the childish imitations a mile away."

"So you say. And, these?"

"Not so much value there, just stuff I've owned over the years."

"You're a hoarder."

He laughed. "You found me out. Now, tell me what I can do for you?"

Holly swallowed. *Let me fall into your arms? Spend every*

night gazing at the stars beside me, perhaps?

She quickly shook off the direction of those thoughts.

"I think it might be what I can do for you." She paused. If it ever got out what she was about to do, not only would she be drummed out of the Reaper business, she might even be brought up on charges.

But, something was terribly wrong and she couldn't live with herself if she didn't at least try to set things right.

"Go on," he said. His expression darkened and he narrowed his eyes at her. His sudden 'all business' manner took her by surprise.

"I shouldn't be here, Reaping you."

There. She'd said it. Right or wrong, it felt good to finally speak her mind.

"What are you saying?"

He leaned closer and Holly got the first realization of how dangerous this man could be. She could feel the clouds of magical energy gathering around them.

"It isn't right. Any of it."

He sat back, obviously relieved. "I knew it."

"You did?" She let out a breath. Then, it wasn't just her. She knew it wasn't ideal to be on the same side as her subject for any issue, but somehow securing his agreement felt appropriate.

"I'm not sure I should be sharing this with you."

It wasn't that she didn't trust him, she thought. She just didn't know him. And, if a girl was going to throw away her whole career and possibly her life — if she was wrong, serious jail time could be involved — she had to make sure he was on the up and up as well.

He sent her a knowing look. "I understand your job hangs in the balance, but my life does as well. Let me reiterate. I'm not ready to die."

"Right." She smiled. "I don't want you to, either. Of

course, as a Reaper, it's not unusual for me to feel that way."

"Really? I thought you were all about being professional and doing your job?"

"I was," she said. "I am. But, that doesn't mean I don't feel anything. My typical case, for instance. A lovely, elderly woman who'd lived a long, full life. Her first grandchild was due any day and it was her time. She begged me to let her at least see the baby born."

"Did you?"

Holly looked down at her hands. "That's not the way it works. It wasn't up to me. Birth and death are their own entities. I only Reap the souls. I've no say when, where, or how they go. She was blessed that she got to die in her sleep."

"But, she didn't see her grandchild born, did she?"

"She didn't." She looked up then, searching his expression for some hint of understanding. "But even if she had, she would have had no time to be with the child. No time to watch it grow into an adult. No time for weddings or births of future grandchildren. So, what good would it have done?"

"None," he said at last.

She shook her head. "And, that's not the worst of them..."

Holly tried to hold back her emotions and it took every bit of her strength to keep the pain of her last Reap from overwhelming her yet again.

"I see."

She sniffled. "I'm a good person. A just person. A fair person. Just not a very good Reaper."

He sat back in his chair. "I disagree. You are the very best person to be a Reaper, because if you don't have feelings for those under your care, who will? Certainly, not the

High Council."

Dabbing at her eyes, she nodded. "Thank you for under-standing."

He smiled at her and reaching across the desk, taking her hand. "Now, tell me what's got you so worried and then I'll tell you what I know."

"I shouldn't be the one Reaping you."

Max felt the hopeful atmosphere deflate around him. She'd not exactly confirmed what he'd hoped.

She wasn't supposed to be the one to Reap him? Not, 'there's been a mistake and you're free to continue living.'

"Go on," was all he managed, doing his best to hide his disappointment.

She chewed her bottom lip and despite his dangerous predicament, he wondered what it would be like to kiss that lip. To press his mouth against hers and revel in the feeling of her mouth against his, his body against hers...

Damn. It was happening again. He was getting terribly distracted. Looking down at his desktop, he fought to rein in his emotions.

Not an easy thing to do for a guy who'd been alone as long as he'd been.

"Anyway, the High Council thinks I'm very good at my job. Stellar at it, according to my last evaluation. All of my subjects are happy with my performance, if not the fact that they think they were unfairly taken."

"You can't really blame them," he muttered, himself feeling pretty much the same way.

"Oh, I don't. Anyway, as good as they say I am, I'm not one of the heavy hitters. I don't do celebrities, gov-ernment officials, royalty, and, um, special beings. Like yourself. Whether you know it or not, you rank up there with Elvis Presley, or Michael Jackson..."

He held up his hand. "I get it. And, I'm flattered... sort of."

"You should be."

"So, you're not the right person to take me. Don't you think you maybe just got a promotion, or something?"

"Reapers don't get promoted. Where the Council hires you is pretty much where you stay. That's what so strange about all this."

"I see. Not that I'm an Immortal? That doesn't strike you as a bit odd?"

She gave him a sheepish smile. "Everybody dies, Mr. Hyland. That's what the ages have told us. Granted, true Immortals are a rare thing. But, even they eventually succumb to something. If not a physical accident, or perhaps a plague, they die in battle. It's been documented."

"Or, they kill each other," he said at the last. "You know, like that old movie and TV show?"

"I don't know about that. I'm not into popular trends. But, either way, you're a pretty important man. One of the Council members should be here Reaping you. Not me."

"Right." He cleared his throat. "There is one other way an Immortal can buy the farm, you know."

"There is? How?"

"If another, more powerful being puts a hit on him."

He watched realization dawn on her. "I don't know... I suppose it's possible."

"It's more than possible. I had a visit from someone I trust more than anyone living or dead. He told me that there was a contract out for my death."

"Holy cow. That can't be legal."

He laughed at the absurdity of it. "Not everyone magical is on the up and up."

She leaned forward. "You think this is an Underworld issue?"

He shrugged. "I doubt it. Those people have an agenda all their own and believe me, I've no part in it. It's not for wealth or privilege either, because I have neither of those."

"Then why kill you?"

"That's what I was trying to figure out when you came in." He pointed to the volume on the desk before him. "I was hoping to find my answers in here."

"What's that?"

"It's my life."

"Your diary?"

He grimaced. "My journal. When you say diary, it makes me sound like a sixteen-year-old girl."

"Sorry. You think the answer is in your past?"

"It must be. I have no enemies presently."

She sat back. "Are you really sure? Because there are a lot of bat-crap crazy people out there, magical and otherwise."

"I've been gleaning the last century and I've found nothing outstanding."

"Well, it occurs to me that it has to be someone pretty important to have filed a death request with the Council and have it sanctioned. Pretty high indeed."

He sat back searching his memory. "The truth is, I've led such a nondescript, boring life, I can't fathom anyone from my past that would go to so much trouble to order my demise."

"Are you sure?"

"Well, I've not gone through all of the volumes, but pretty sure."

She crossed her arms. "We need to be really sure. Because, if not, it's likely politically motivated. Or, maybe someone who wants you dead to prove something."

"No offense, but it sounds pretty farfetched to me. Still,

I wouldn't mind at all if you'd like to help me with the search. Two pair of eyes have to be better than one, right?"

"Right. But, only until this evening. My mentor should be arriving on the late train. I promised to meet with him."

"I'd forgotten about that."

She looked at him, and while he wasn't a sympathy junkie, he enjoyed the expression she gave him.

"Why don't you come with me? If anyone can figure this all out, it's him."

"Are you sure? I mean, do you think it's safe to tell anyone about this?"

"I think it's safe to tell him. As I hear it, it's a forced retirement sort of thing. I've heard it's not an arrangement he's happy about. He'd be the last one running to the High Council."

"So, maybe he won't be pulling the Reaping cord on me, right?"

"Not at all. Besides, I've only asked him to advise me. Even though he is way above me in management, no Reaper can just take over another's client. It must be freely given. I'd never do that if there was a valid reason not to. Like if somehow one of the higher ups had made a mistake."

"Then that's a possibility, then?" Max tried to keep the hopeful tone from his voice.

"Not really," she said, casting her gaze downwards. "I mean, it's never happened before."

"There's a first time for everything, right?"

"I guess. But, I don't want you to get your hopes up. It's such a remote possibility..."

He took her hands in his and gently squeezed. "Don't worry about me. Anyway, I have even more reason to want to stay alive now. I was thinking that you and I might, you know, get together."

She suddenly flashed a stunned expression. "Together, how?"

"Like this," he said. Leaning forward, he pulled her toward him and kissed her. To his surprise, for the briefest of seconds, she kissed him back. Her touch was timid at first, and then he suddenly had the impression that she wanted more. A lot more.

But, at the last minute, as if she'd suddenly remembered who and what she was, she jerked back from him. Her face turned from porcelain pale to immediate fire engine red.

"Oh, dear. We shouldn't have done that," she muttered, scooting back from him.

"Why not?"

Her eyes brimmed with tears and he saw her bottom lip quiver. "Because, even if somehow you survive, we can never be a...a..."

"Couple?"

She nodded. "It's not a good idea for a Reaper to get involved in romantic entanglements. Ever."

Max crossed his arms and sat back. "Reapers can't fall in love? Why not? Even with other Reapers?"

She swallowed and then crossed her arms in front of her, as though the air had turned frigid. "With anyone. Let's just say, with pressures of the job, months on the road, and so on — it never ends well."

She shrugged and the look of misery she wore nearly broke his heart.

He leaned toward her again, and again gently touched her hands. "We have so much against me even surviving this travesty, why don't we put away worrying over falling in love until after we solve our immediate problem. Then, if we manage to work things out, we'll go from there.

Deal?"

She nodded and the expression of panic and misery started to recede. "Deal," she said at last, clearly doing her best to send him a halfhearted smile.

While it wasn't a rigning endorsement, Max was thrilled to see it. Damn the fates that caused this all. He was going to beat them at this, somehow, some way.

"Good. Now, let's do this," he said, handing her the volume that held his sixteenth century memoirs.

It was as simple as that. For the first time in centuries he'd not only opened himself to another person, he trusted her with his past. That, on the relationship scale was akin to moving from a first date in a coffee shop to sharing an apartment and picking out curtains.

In other words, whether she could accept it or not, they were united in their quest. Like it or not, they were now a couple. Of sorts.

Heaven help him, Max rather liked it.

Master Georges Renault watched the landscape slip by his window with very little thought to scenery. Seated in the luxury car of the Roundhouse LTD, he could have cared less that he crossed principalities to get to his destination. After all, geography was more the concern of man rather than Magics.

In fact, he only cared about one thing — his destination. He'd vacationed in Nocturne Falls once and had found it too 'touristy' for his liking. As a man who'd traveled the world for better than a millennium, he much preferred his own properties to that of the masses. In fact, other than seeing others across the existential planes, he'd had little care for his subjects.

Whether beings lived or died had simply been a function of his profession. When his job was finished, he preferred to return to his mountain cabin in the Andes, or the lovely grotto in South America. Anywhere that he didn't have to deal with the mewling, miserable beings that walked the planet around him.

One of the first Reapers, he'd a long, distinguished history of collecting souls. Napoleon had been one of his favorites, as had Attila the Hun, and James Dean — although to be true, he hadn't understood the importance of the movie star's passing. He'd barely been a blip on the face of history.

Still, it wasn't the quality of his Reaping that made him boil with anger. It was the fact that they'd had the audacity to throw him away like yesterday's nuclear waste. He was more than that. He could have gone on Reaping for two, maybe three more centuries.

One little mistake with a presidential assassination and that movie star that everyone hated but wouldn't admit to hating, and there it was. Put him out to pasture, send him to the great beyond and abandon him to the ages.

More than that, after his many years of faithful service, they'd had the audacity to deny him a seat on the High Council.

They'd be sorry for that.

"My lord," his valet, Cravens, said as he held out the latest issue of the New York Times to him. "Something to read, perhaps?"

As far as underlings went, Cravens was the best of the best. It had been a coup, two hundred years earlier when Renault had acquired the man. Though, a third-generation warlock was not that much of an acquisition. He'd been way overpriced at the time and his abilities rather mediocre. But, he was very good at summoning spirits, fetching the newspaper and taking care of Renault's wardrobe. Oh, and for scheming. The man was a far better planner than the old Reaper had ever dreamed of being.

"I don't feel like reading right now."

"Of course, my lord. Is there something else I can get you? I saw there were a couple of very lovely ladies in the coach behind us that could use some company. I'm sure I could coax them to come visit with us. It would help pass the time since we're about four hours from Nocturne Falls."

Renault waved him off. The man was practically a walking hormone. Yes, it had been fun scoring dates with him over the years. Mostly bathing beauties and models were to his tastes. Having chosen a persona as a young Dean Martin, Cravens had gotten more than his share of female companions.

"Not now. We have bigger fish to catch." He thought a moment. Perhaps a little more incentive was what was needed here. "And, if things go well, there's a sweet little Reaper girl that might need some consoling later."

"Really, my lord?"

"Help me get what I want and she's all yours. I promise."

"I'm your man, sir."

Renault smiled. It was a pity, really. Holly Dent had been one of the finest Reapers he'd ever apprenticed. So, serious about her work and a depth of empathy for her subjects that went far beyond what most Reapers possessed. She was a jewel, to be sure. Add to that, a lovely creature. She was a diamond of the first water, though he doubted she knew it.

Of course, giving such a lovely woman to his servant as a plaything was a bit unsettling. Renault knew well that Cravens didn't always play nice with his toys. Well, that was a rather broad generalization. His last five relationships hadn't ended well for the young women involved. The unsettling part was, Cravens preferred it that way.

Pushing aside any thoughts for Ms. Dent, he instead ruminated on just how high up the High Council corporate ladder he was about to ascend.

And once he was there, it was going to be a completely different game. They would be bowing to his rule and he would own them all, buying and selling lives as he pleased. They didn't yet know it, but the world of Magics was about to change forever.

Master Georges Renault was going to be at the pinnacle of it all.

CHAPTER SIX

HOLLY COULDN'T HELP HERSELF. SHE stretched and yawned. The sun was setting and Mr. Hyland had just put the light on. Refocusing on the pages in front of her, she became aware of several things at once.

First, sitting curled up in a desk chair was not the best choice of positions for studying the massive tome in front of her. When she moved, her bones creaked like she was a ninety-year old woman.

Second, that though he'd been quiet for the last three hours the man spoke volumes by the cadence of his breathing, the small noises he made when he came across something that interested him, and the alluring scent of his cologne. While it wasn't overpowering, there was just a hint of it in the air and Holly enjoyed the crisp, clean smell of it.

She wondered if he knew just how desirable he was. Probably, she told herself. Besides, how many drop dead gorgeous men were out there that didn't at least have some inkling of how they affected the ladies?

Shaking her head, she went back to her reading. If he knew she was thinking such thoughts, she'd be in deep, deep water for sure.

"Well," he asked, settling back in his chair. "See anything?"

She'd only made it through about fifty years' worth — a lot for her but not so much for him, really.

"One major thing. You've led a pretty boring life."

"Exactly what I said. We can keep looking, of course, but I'm telling you, it's pretty much all the same. I got up. I took a shower. I met with the president of Harvard University. Blah, blah, blah..."

"Well, your list of acquaintances is pretty impressive, but still not anything that should make you a target."

He let out a breath. "This is getting us nowhere. What time does your mentor friend arrive?"

She looked down at her watch. "A little over an hour from now."

"Then what's say we clean up, head out and grab a bite before we meet him? I know a sweet little eatery about a block from the train station."

"Sounds like a plan. Let me get my clothes together."

"Oh, and your bird can come, too, if you want."

She shook her head. "No way. Artemis hates Master Renault. Says he's a pretentious old goat. They've never gotten along."

"Gotcha. It'll just be the two of us."

She hesitated not sure if she should mention the other person who would be with her former mentor. "Master Renault usually travels with his valet."

"Valet? Do people even use them anymore?"

"Master Renault does. He's very picky about his clothing. Wait until you see him. You'll understand."

He shrugged. "Okay."

"Oh, and there's one other thing."

"Another servant?"

"No, about Cravens. He's kind of a creep. Well, not kind of. He's the kind of being that makes your skin crawl. Well, my skin, anyways."

"Is he human?"

"He's a Warlock, but not a very nice one."

"Seems odd that he chooses to be a servant. Warlocks are usually alpha beings."

She held out her hand to him. "Don't tell anyone I told you this, but rumor is he lost most of his power after an altercation with one of the members of the High Council's family. I don't know any details, but I've heard it was bad. All the official records have been sealed."

"Wow. All this makes me glad I've never involved myself in politics. Too much insanity." Rising from his desk, he walked around and opened the door for her.

"I'll see you in ten minutes," she told him and headed toward the stairs. Of course, she felt his gaze on her back as she walked away.

Ordinarily, she'd be annoyed at getting a man's notice so blatantly. But with the Immortal, it was different somehow. She found herself enjoying his attention and stood a little straighter.

"There is one other thing," he said just as she reached the stairwell.

She turned back to look at him. "Yes?"

"Please call me Max. I beg you. I hate my surname. My father was so not a nice person and every time you call me Mr. Hyland it reminds me of the old man."

She grinned. "I'll call you Max, but only if you call me Holly."

"It would be my pleasure," he said, bowing low.

Her mood lightened and she headed up the stairs. Fates help her, she was liking this guy.

But, deep down, warning bells were ringing like a five-alarm fire. He was her subject, after all. She was courting trouble of epic proportions.

Could this be what she'd been missing? Not just a man

in her life, but this man. Something about him drew her like a moth to a flame. Heaven help her, she couldn't deny that she wanted to learn all there was about him, too.

If it was a mistake, then so be it. Wasn't a girl entitled to a mistake once in a while? Because, what if it wasn't? It had only been a day, after all. She couldn't wait to see what tomorrow would bring.

"You're in a good mood," Artemis said as she slipped into her room.

"I am. Maybe for the first time in a long time."

The bird ruffled its feathers. "I'm happy for you, but I'm a little concerned."

"I'm a big girl, you know."

"Yes, but it's not like you to be so impulsive. Do you really like this guy?"

"I do."

The bird chuckled. "Really? And you're sure he hasn't slipped something into your water?"

Holly let out a breath. "I doubt it. Besides, I'd be able to tell. You know I'm extra careful about that kind of thing."

It wouldn't be the first time someone had tried to take out a Reaper. She'd been offered anything from poisoned muffins to being locked in a carbon monoxide filled garage.

"Still. This one is different."

"He is. And, I like him, Artie. Really like him."

"That's a record for you then. I've never seen you get interested in a guy before. Let alone, practically overnight."

"I know, and yes, it's scary. But, it's thrilling and so exciting. I know I sound like a giddy schoolgirl, but this guy is so awesome."

"And, he's also marked for death."

There it was. Her heart nearly broke.

"I know."

"No one I know is better at figuring things out than you," Artemis said. "But, the time may come for you to tell him good-bye."

There was nothing more to be said. She grabbed her sweater and told her friend that they were going to get a meal and then meet Master Renault at the train station.

"For what it's worth," the bird told her as Holly reached for the door's knob. "I'm pulling for you. I hope the two of you figure it all out. You, more than anyone I've ever known, deserve happiness."

The drive to the restaurant was filled with quiet anxiety on both their parts. Max made a few attempts at conversation, but a new wall had come up between them and he wasn't quite sure what it was.

"This seems an odd choice of a car," the Reaper remarked as they slowly made their way to the eatery.

"What? It's a converted hearse. I don't do pick-ups, anymore. Plus, it's size alone makes it the best car to get through these crowds, right?"

Because of the growing arrivals for the week-long festival, traffic was slow and it was taking twice as long to get to the restaurant. Finally, when they pulled into Chang's, he couldn't help letting out a long breath.

"Listen," Holly said, placing her hand on his arm. "I know this is a strange situation. I don't mean to be off putting, but what if we're wrong?"

"About my dying? I don't think so."

"What if it's just a mistake from the higher ups?"

He smiled at her. "Weren't you the one who said the Council doesn't make mistakes? That, whatever they decree is law?"

She shifted in her seat. "I did, but you know, it's not out

of the realm of possibility."

"No, it isn't. Someone has convinced them that for the betterment of the world — magical and human — that my number is up."

"It's not right," she said at last.

Max had a hint of what was bothering her. She cared about him. While he wasn't sure if a Reaper's crush was a good thing, he did warm to the idea. The more they were together, the more he wanted to learn more about her.

And protect her.

"If they're right and I must go, then what will you do?"

She looked at him then and he saw her eyes cloud with emotion. It was a struggle to be sure. To go against the High Council meant a severe penalty. Loss of her Reaper privileges, imprisonment or worse? Definite possibilities.

"I won't let them take you without a fight."

There it was. The words he'd ached to hear from her and yet ones that shook him to his marrow.

"I thank you, but if it comes down to it, I want you to back away."

"Why?"

He let out another breath. "You're a good person, Holly. I learned that today. No one else in my life has ever put in that kind of effort for me. I appreciate all you've done, but if it means your life as well, then don't risk it."

He felt her eyes on his face, studying him, measuring what he was about.

"It's my life. I'll do what I think is right. For an innocent man to be put down for no reason, is unthinkable. I've stood beside many making the transition, and even when it tore my heart out to do so, I knew that it was the right thing."

"I don't know how you do it, stay by them when..."

She leaned over. "I can't imagine anyone ever having

to die alone. It's possible, you know, even when there's a room full of people. That's the reason I chose this profession."

"Of course. I never meant to judge you."

"It's okay. People mostly don't understand what I do."

A moment passed between them.

"How about we grab some take-out and head to the train station?"

She nodded. "Sounds like a plan."

They went into the quaint little restaurant and Max couldn't help but enjoy the decor. Beaded curtains hung from the walkways, shelf after shelf of intricately painted ceramics and jade carvings adorned the walls. It was a Chinese take-out heaven.

After perusing the menu, and ordering their meal, Max paid for their feast and after receiving the multiple containers motioned Holly to the door.

"I know the perfect place to eat our meal," he said. "Do you trust me?"

For the briefest moment, he watched a series of emotions play across her face. Surprise, doubt and then decision had warred for her thoughts. But when she looked up at him, the planes of her face relaxed and a tiny grin tugged at her mouth.

"I do."

Max let out a breath he didn't know he was holding. "Great. There's a park across from the train station. Come on."

Rather than move the car, they walked the short distance to the park and just at dusk, the town's party decorations began to light up. Motioning her toward a picnic table, he sat the food down. She handed him his drink, and they settled themselves.

"Very nice," she said with a grin.

He let out a breath. "It's one of my favorite places. I love the lights, the fountain, and most people are waiting on tables at the other eating establishments we are enjoying the nice evening.

"I love it here," she said, and then shot him a surprised expression. "Sorry, that slipped out."

It was his turn to smile back at her. "Think nothing of it. Nocturne Falls is an easy place to love. Supernaturals and humans alike. There's just something about the place." It was true. He'd been drawn here years earlier and not once had he considered going anywhere else.

"I don't know about settling down," she said, after sipping her tea. "I've been on the road without stopping for so long, to be in one place is almost unimaginable."

"I'm sure." He leaned forward. "But have you considered staying in one place?"

She let out a breath. "What would I do? Reaping is all I know."

"You could learn another trade, perhaps start a business, you're a smart, accomplished woman."

He watched her face flush a little and knew he'd struck a nerve.

"I suppose so, but to be honest, I've never wanted to do anything else."

"Of course."

A moment of silence passed between them. Max finished his drink and pushed his food aside. Suddenly, his appetite had vanished and the pressing anvil of reality settled in his thoughts.

That was when he felt her hand on his arm.

"I'm sorry. I know it sounds bad. I mean, what kind of person am I that lives every day in the shadow of death? But, it's who I am."

He nodded. "You've nothing to be sorry for. None of us

can help what we are."

"Thank you for understanding."

Finishing his drink, he stood and started gathering the remainder of their meal. "What do you say we take it home? Or, shall we pitch the rest?"

"I hate to waste such lovely food. Why don't we see what we can salvage for a midnight snack later?"

He nodded. "I'm glad you're into leftovers."

Once they'd put everything back in the bag, he held out his arm to her and they walked to the train station, chatting pleasantly about the weather, the town and even their choice in music.

Nothing more was said about her job, his future or even what they might do the next day. Like slipping into a new suit, the stiff, unemotional tone returned to their voices. Though, he hadn't meant it to happen, the change between them felt as if someone had opened a window and let the warm air out of the room.

Holly knew the exact moment when her disappointment reached its lowest point. One moment they were sharing a wonderful dinner, enjoyable conversation and the crisp feeling of a new relationship.

She hadn't felt that comfortable with anyone in a very long time. She remembered her first high school crush, and yes, though she felt foolish thinking that way, it was like that.

What's wrong with me? she'd asked herself on more than one occasion, but this time, it was beyond thinkable.

"Here we are," he said at last. "Do you know which train he's arriving on?"

Pushing back her misery, Holly pulled out her cell phone. "Here it is. The one from Cincinnati."

He motioned her to a bench. They were about twenty

minutes early and suddenly, time stretched out like a deep canyon between them.

"It's been awhile since I've toured the town. This is quite nice."

"I love the decor."

It was true. An early American design, it was a cavernous waiting area, with polished wood benches, one long mahogany counter, surrounded by stained glass with gas lighting all around.

"It's odd, you know. Most people either drive or fly. But taking a train seems odd but quaint."

"I don't care for flying," Holly told him. "Driving would be fun, but since I travel so much I really can't afford a car. And, Artie doesn't like to fly. She gets nervous and her feathers start falling out."

Max laughed and she liked the sound of it. He had a deep, throaty sound.

Darn it. The man was too adorable by half. It was too easy to fall into the fantasy of a relationship with a guy like him. Them together taking long afternoon walks, enjoying early morning coffee and sharing the newspaper, or dining together at one of Nocturne Fall's quaint eateries. And, then, snuggled together in bed, soft caresses, heated kisses — and so much more.

"Everything okay?"

Suddenly back in the present, Holly felt her face heat up. "Sorry, just got lost in my thoughts for a moment."

He leaned over and touched her chin. "Must be something pretty fascinating to take you so far away."

"Not really. Just, possibilities."

"Then, whatever it is, I hope it works out for you."

And that's when she knew she was doomed.

"I do too."

They were so close now. Nose to nose. Breath to breath.

Holly's heart beat faster and her breath came short. Part of her wanted to fall into his arms, to once again taste his kiss, to forget everything and just melt into his embrace. And, she probably would have too, if the train whistle hadn't sounded announcing the next train's arrival.

"I guess your friend is arriving."

"Right."

The spell between them was broken for sure. But, as they stood up, he held his arm out for her. "May I escort you?"

Smiling, she agreed. "Thank you."

It was a short walk to the gate and they watched as people started to disembark from the train.

"So," he started. "This friend of yours. You never told me very much about him. Well, other than he dresses well, is extremely old and has a creepy henchman."

Reality hit her like a ton of bricks. Fate had taken over both of them and there was nothing she could do to stop it. The one man who would accomplish what she could not. It was time to put away her ridiculous thoughts and face up to what lie ahead.

"I have a confession to make," she told him, her heart suddenly squeezing in her chest.

He tilted his head, and she saw the hint of disappointment lingering in his eyes. "I know whatever you've done, it's because you had to."

"I told him I was giving up the Reap. Giving you to him." she said. "Of course, now I know you better. I won't do it but he'll do his best to convince me that it'll be for the best."

"There's my girl," a familiar voice said behind her. "So good to see you again."

A stab of pain went through her and she wished that she'd never come to this magical place. Or, that she'd never become a Reaper in the first place.

Under any other circumstances, she knew that Max was a man she could spend eternity with.

But now it was impossible.

"Master Renault," she said, doing her best to keep the emotion from her voice. "This is Maximillian Hyland. He's the Immortal I was sent to Reap."

And just like that, the being who'd taken her under his wing so many years earlier, who'd taught her everything about Reaping and encouraged her still to that day with birthday cards and letters of encouragement, stood before her.

Around six-foot tall, Master Renault was lean and slightly stooped over. He had a squarish face, silver hair and a rather thick mustache. But, instead of exuding the presence of the powerful mage he was, her former mentor instead gave off the vibes of a friendly grandfather. He even walked with a cane.

Of course, she knew that he could run faster and jump higher than most twenty-year-old athletes.

Why he'd chosen to retreat into such an elderly, helpless identity had been quite the surprise. There were some that said for a Reaper, he'd barely reached middle age.

But, their profession was not an easy one, and the weight of it was far heavier than most physical beings could even attempt, let alone master.

A huge grin spread across his face when he saw her, showing a mouth full of perfectly white teeth with a single gold tooth in the front. He also wore his traditional opaque monocle in his right eye. The legend was that he'd taken on one of the most dangerous Reaps of all time, another powerful Reaper, in fact, and had lost his eye in the final struggle.

But, none of that history was apparent now, as he'd taken

on the guise of a kindly older gentleman.

"Ah, the stubborn one, eh?"

Max didn't even look at Holly but instead stepped forward. "Ordinarily, I'd greet you with a handshake, but I believe it'd be safer for me to not get too cozy here. Seeing as you might take my attempt at cordiality as death wish."

The older man laughed. "Of course. But, what's done is done, young man. Unfortunately, you're only putting off the inevitable."

"Really?"

"Indeed. Holly is an excellent clinician, but she doesn't have the strongest of powers when it comes to the really big jobs."

"So, I take it, Reaping healthy young Immortals is more your speed? Rather than ninety-year-old humans in nursing homes?"

Holly stepped forward, suddenly aware that they were drawing attention. "Gentlemen," she started. "I think we should take this conversation elsewhere."

The two men squared off, Max to her left and Master Renault to her right. Holly literally felt the electricity building in the air around them.

"I suppose that's wise," Master Georges said at last. "Wouldn't want to cause a scene in public, now would we?"

Max crossed his arms. "I know the local sheriff and they don't take kindly to bad press."

"Understood. Shall we go?" Holly wanted to get the two of them as far away from each other as possible.

Renault nodded. "Of course. My man is retrieving my luggage and we can be off."

He turned and walked to the car where the suitcases were being loaded onto carts.

She turned back to Max, who now stood stone still, staring after the Reaper. She could see by his tight expression that all of his congeniality was gone.

"Max, I'm truly sorry."

He didn't look at her, but kept his gaze trained on the old man.

"I hope you won't mind finding a ride back to the funeral home. It shouldn't be hard to get a taxi since it's still early."

"What about you?"

He did look down at her then. "I find I'm no longer in a mood for company." He let out a breath. "Please, go on without me. I feel the need to be on my own a bit."

With that, he turned and walked away. She saw by the way he held himself tall and stiff that whatever friendship or connection they'd formed was now over.

She didn't blame him. He was in a fight to stay alive.

Reality slammed against her like a wrecking ball on the side of a building. She'd do all she could to save him. Go against the High Council if she had to. Surely, they would see the error they'd committed.

After that was done, she'd go back to being a Reaper and he'd be just another client. It was how it was supposed to be. Then, she'd go on to another city, another job. Her problem here would be solved.

She should have been cheering, happy that Maximillian Hyland would live.

So why did it feel like someone just ripped her heart out of her chest?

CHAPTER SEVEN

"THE GAME IS ON," MAX said as he stepped out into the night. Pulling up his collars against the wind, he hastened his steps meaning to put as much distance as possible between himself and that ancient Reaper. "Kindly old gentleman, my foot."

Picking up his pace, he went to the one place where he was sure he could find an ally. Of course, he and his twin couldn't exactly be called friends, but they were two of a kind, so to speak, so if anyone could help him figure things out, it was Matty.

A steady rain had just begun to fall when he arrived at the infamous biker bar night club, Howlers. Ducking inside the darkened club, he took a moment for his vision to adjust. Fortunately, that wasn't too long, since he felt every eye in the room land on him.

The usual crowd was gathered. A couple of bikers were playing pool in the next room, two women sat arm in arm at one end of the bar. And assorted tables were filled with every sort from suit and tie bad boy wannabes to some of the local talent. Werewolves and vampires were among the majority, but a few humans had wandered in wanting to prove that they had the stones to even come to one of the most edgy clubs in Nocturne Falls.

"Hey, stranger," the bartender called from behind the

bar. "Long time no see."

He sent her a respectful nod and took a seat that didn't have him too close to any of her other patrons. There was only one person he wanted to mix it up with tonight.

"Can I get a shot of Patron?"

"Holy cow," she said, sending him a wide-eyed shocked expression. "Who died?"

He let out a huff. "Nobody. Yet."

She set his drink in front of him and stood back. "Um, before you try to run up a tab, you need to know that last week I had to throw your brother out. He was trying to pick a fight with one of the local vamps who bet him that he couldn't make enough blood to survive a good feeding. Damn near killed him, too."

He waved her off. "I know, too much alcohol even for an Immortal is not a good thing. I only want this one and then a glass of tonic water to nurse the rest of the night."

"Sure thing. So, what has you gracing us with your presence."

"I need to talk to my brother. Did you ban him after his bout of bad judgement?"

She gave him a dry laugh. "No. But I should have. That guy was really ticked off that I wouldn't let them finish their wager. But, if Matty boy come back in here with any more harebrained ideas, I might not be inclined to intervene."

As if summoned by magic, Matty appeared, wearing his faux biker clothes with his little witch ladies on each side of him. He stopped short when he saw Max sitting at the bar.

"What the hell?"

Pulling his girls in, he whispered something at them and then sent them on their way.

"Brother," Max said, after he threw back the shot of

tequila.

His brother crossed his arms and stood back a minute. "Be still my heart. My big brother in a bar and partaking in booze, too? Is this Armageddon? Something cataclysmic must be about to go down."

Max cleared his throat. "I don't like this any more than you do. But, I'm in bad trouble and unfortunately, there's not a soul I can turn to except you."

Suddenly, his brother's sarcastic expression changed. Every doubt clouded his sapphire gaze and his face paled visibly. There was only one explanation for that.

Fear.

It didn't matter if the two were fast friends or mortal enemies, there was a connection between them and though each had tried to free himself from the other on more than one occasion it always came back to one thing. Kill one, and the other would perish.

Max knew that his brother's concern wasn't for anyone's benefit but his own, but that didn't bother him too much. Although, he liked to think that despite their differences, Matty valued his brother's existence beyond the thought of his own mortality.

"Spill," was all he said after waving off the waitress.

"I have another guest coming to the manse. Another Reaper, in fact. One of their muckety-muck higher ups, I think."

"What makes you say that? Was he wearing a badge, or something."

"Let's just say it's how he looked at me, you know, much the same way you look at the cow when you're about to sit down at a steak dinner."

His brother blew out a puff of air. "That is bad news."

"No kidding."

"So, he tried to take you already?"

Max shook his head. "Thankfully, no. We were in public and there was no accident or anything that could justify my sudden death. Too many non-magical people about, I'd imagine."

"So, let me get this straight. After you invited one Reaper into your home, pop, another one shows up and you say, I dunno, 'Why don't you come have a sleepover at my house? It'll be fun?'"

Scowling, Max crossed his arms to keep from doing bodily harm to his sibling. "It wasn't like that. Holly doesn't look like she could harm a flea, and…"

"Wait. The Reaper is a chick?"

Max did his best to clamp down on his temper. Not just at Matty, but at himself as well. "I know it sounds bad, but nothing can be done about it now."

"Is she cute?"

"Breathtaking, but that's not the point…"

"Ha! A beautiful woman wants you dead but that's not the point? Bro, you disappoint me."

"Will you please get serious? The fact is, she's a good person, aside from her choice of profession, that is. She's a Reaper because she cares about people. Wants to ease their passing."

"So, a friendly Reaper. That's just perfect."

"All I'm saying is she's a good person and I doubt she bore me any ill intentions — especially once we became more acquainted."

Matty sat back. "Oh, you sly dog," he snickered. "Just how 'acquainted' did the two of you become?"

His stomach clenched at his brother's insinuation. "Not that much. I mean, we barely even kissed…"

"Oh, yeah right. You are either a liar or a fool, my bro."

Glad that he didn't have the propensity for blushing, Max waved his hands. "You're off track. Can we please get back to my problem? That is, unless you want to join me in a dirt nap."

Matty cleared his throat. "Right. Let's get serious. What can you tell me about the new guy?"

"I'll do better than tell you," Max said, pulling his phone out of his jacket pocket and handing it to his brother. "I took a snap of him when he got off the train."

"Right."

Max held his breath for a moment, hoping his brother would not just understand, but also see the importance of this new development.

"Wow," Matty cleared his throat. "What are you thinking?"

Max let out a breath. "I think his arrival has signed our death warrant, that's what I think."

"There are rules."

"Rules?" Max shrugged. "I beginning to think they're more like guidelines."

Matty let out a breath. "Well, I've not gone against any mandates, lately, have you?"

Max dropped his gaze to his clenched fists on the table in front of him. It was the one question he didn't want to answer, but he had no choice.

"Not lately," Max said after a moment. Closing his eyes, he recited the words his father had taught him centuries earlier.

"Immortals can go on living if they don't do three things. Harm a magical. Harm themselves..."

"Or harm a human," Matty finished his sentence. "My god, Max. Tell me you didn't..."

That was when he realized exactly why he was about to be Reaped. It happened a long time ago. A very long time ago. Before he knew he was immortal. Before he even knew the rules.

Max lifted his face and looked his brother straight in the eyes. "I can't lie. I am guilty of harming a human. But, I didn't just harm him. I killed him..."

Holly looked up from her lap. She was sitting in the back seat of the taxi with her oldest friend and mentor. She should have been happy to see him. She should have been laughing and reflecting on old times. But, somehow, when Max left her, all the gleeful anticipation did too.

Well, that wasn't entirely true. And, to be honest, she didn't blame him for bolting. After all, Master Renault was the one Reaper in all the realm of magic who could end him. With a drop of his hand, in the space of a breath, the Immortal would be forever gone from this plane of existence.

Moreover, though it had been the one thing she'd come to Nocturne Falls to do, she'd been dreading it almost since her arrival.

"You like him, don't you?" Renault said.

Suddenly her mouth went dry. To be called out so suddenly for something she'd thought very protected inside of her, well, that was downright unsettling.

"I beg your pardon, Master Renault, but how I feel has no effect on my mission. Isn't that what you taught me?"

He laughed. "A lesson you well remember."

"I remember all you taught me."

"Even the things you don't agree with?" he let out a breath. "It's all right for you to disagree with me."

She watched him for a moment. "All right, but not proper. After all, you are one of the oldest Reapers in the realm. Your teachings must be right."

He nodded. "Oh, they are. But, as you said, they were my teachings. My body of experience, knowledge and beliefs. Still, you do well to follow them."

"Yes. I know." Holly looked down at her hands again. "But, teacher, what if you know the mission is wrong?"

His eyes narrowed in contemplation and he sent her a sharp stare and she felt the cut of it on her skin.

"Is that what you think about the Immortal? That he transcends your mission somehow? Or, is it your betters who don't know what they're doing?"

Though his tone was soft, it scraped on her skin like dull razor. "No, it's not that at all..."

"Isn't it?"

She let out a breath, and then another. "Perhaps it is. And, I'm not ashamed to say it, but Mr. Hyland is a decent man. He cares for others and serves human and nonhuman alike..."

"That has nothing to do with the Council's decision. Perhaps you've forgotten, but it isn't your job to decide who lives and who dies."

Holly swallowed. "I haven't forgotten." She glanced up at him, meeting his gaze. "You're right. I do have feelings for him. Complicated feelings. Is that why I have no power over him? Why I couldn't Reap him the night we met?"

The older man waved her off. "I doubt it. You didn't even know him then. You were just acting as someone with your level of talents and strength would do. He's a powerful being. His abilities are far beyond what the High Council suspected."

"Oh." That did help to lessen her shame, somewhat.

"The question is, can you overcome your feelings to do what must be done? If not, then I am more than happy to get the job done. You will, of course, have to give me permission to do so."

"I know."

Holly watched something alarming slip into his expression. Joy? Eagerness? Or, was it possibly glee?

Whatever it was, it slipped away almost as quickly as it appeared, and the calm, self-assured expression returned, a pleasant countenance that she'd always known him by.

Yes, this was the man she'd known for many years, her teacher and friend. But, who was the other? She didn't know for sure, or even if she'd imagined it. Whatever it was, she felt the danger that now hung in the air between them.

The cab pulled up to the Funeral Home's entrance. She went to open the door, but felt his hand on her arm.

"I hope you don't mind, but I've decided to find lodging elsewhere. I need some distance to clear my thoughts. There are too many shadows of the souls who have passed through those halls still occupying this place."

She tilted her head. "Souls? There's only Mr. Hyland and his cook that I've seen. Oh, and Artemis."

He smiled. "You don't recognize them, do you?"

"Recognize who?"

"The souls of the dead. Those who've been in the undertaker's care at one time or another."

"But, they've gone..."

He shrugged. "They have, but their essence in the air. It can be most distracting. No wonder you haven't been able to concentrate."

"Really?"

"Perhaps you'd like to come stay with me. Clearly the funeral home is a most challenging environment."

Holly bit her lip. Was it possible that it was the funeral home blocking her powers?

As soon as the thought occurred to her, though, Holly knew it wasn't true. Whatever had blocked her Reaper power, it wasn't a pile of bricks and wood. No. It was Max Hyland. She'd felt his strength even when they'd been at dinner.

"I'm already settled in and it's late. Even if the circumstances were different, I'm too tired to do anything right now. I'm sure things will look better in the morning."

He nodded and smiled at her. "As you wish, my dear. I'm here to help however I can."

Holly watched the driver pull away and felt a sudden relief at his leaving. Though, his outer appearance was his usual, pleasant countenance, she couldn't help feeling the undercurrent of frustration that stirred within him.

Or, perhaps she was just imagining all of it. Perhaps she was just weak and inadequate and didn't want to face completing what was turning out to be the most unpleasant assignment she'd ever faced.

She pulled her shawl a bit tighter around her shoulders and a breeze blew around the courtyard, enveloping her with bracing cool air. Just as she turned toward the house, a car pulled into the drive.

At first, she thought it was Max, but it was another man — a man with the same build, the same square jaw and the same long, sexy stride.

"Hello," he waved to her, practically in Max Hyland's voice. "You're that hot chick, Reaper girl, I take it."

Holly's mouth went dry, and a shock of surprise went through her like lighting in a summer storm. "That would be me," she managed.

He sent her a wide, predatory grin. "Awesome. I've been wanting to meet you."

For some reason Holly didn't understand, this man scared her. Oh, sure, he looked very much the same as Max, but then again, totally different. Max was handsome, but in a clever, sophisticated way. He was serious and witty, all at the same time.

But, this guy? The stranger before her was as good looking, too. But, edgy, frightening and, well, dangerous.

If there was one thing Holly had made her life's endeavor, it was to stay away from danger, especially when it came to men.

It was all she could do to keep from running to the house, slamming the door shut and locking it.

"Awesome," he said, leaning back on his car's door.

"Yeah, well, it's late and I need to be getting to bed."

He shrugged. "It's not that late. And, Max should be here pretty soon. I hear he's in a world of trouble."

"I don't think it's proper for us to talk about it. It's his private business after all."

The stranger pushed forward and in three long steps, was standing in front of her. "For the record, I'm his brother and the only family he has on this plane of existence. Max and I are twins."

"I figured as much. But, still. If you'll excuse me."

He shook his head. "I'm sorry, but I don't excuse you. Max is more than just my brother. The two of us are connected. If he dies, I die. And, let me tell you. I'm against dying."

"Everybody is," she said, trying to push past him. He grabbed her arm and pulled her back around.

"You don't understand. I'll do whatever it takes to stay alive. You don't know this, but my brother's no angel. He may deserve to die, but I don't."

Holly didn't know what to say. "I don't know what you're talking about. I just know that he was who I have orders for. If you're part of that, I can't help it. I'm sorry. Now, please let me go."

The man stared hard at her for a few minutes. "Sure, thing, lady." With that he stepped back and threw his hands in the air.

She stumbled back a pace but managed to keep her

footing. "Thank you." She turned back and did her best not to run into the house. She may have been trembling in fear on the inside, but the last thing she wanted was for this stranger to know it.

"For what it's worth, he thinks you're a special lady. That you have a heart and that you actually care for him. Too bad he's wrong."

Finally, Holly entered the house, slamming the door closed behind her, she ran upstairs and into her room. Her chest was tight and she had a hard time catching her breath. Flipping on the bedroom light, she nearly startled Artemis off her perch.

"What the devil?"

Sniffing, Holly turned the lock on the door and then threw herself onto the bed. "It's not the devil, Artie. It's me." Her tears welled up and before she could take another breath she was sobbing. "It's me and I'm a monster."

CHAPTER EIGHT

"DUDE. WHAT WERE YOU THINKING?" Max asked Matty. "He'd just pulled into the drive to see his twin manhandling Holly in the driveway.

Matty threw up his hands. "Back off, bro. I didn't hurt her. And, while we're on it, why are you so worried about her? She wants to kill us, remember?"

Max shoved his brother out of the way. "She wants to kill me. I want to kill you." With that he stormed past him and headed into the house. Just as he got inside the door, he heard her bedroom door slam upstairs.

"Hey, I'm sorry, okay? She's a tough cookie. I know her type. She'll lead you on, and when you least expect it, bam. You're toast and I'll be on the slab next to you."

Max spun around. "You're wrong. You don't know her. She doesn't want to kill anybody. Ever."

"If you're right, she's the worst Reaper in her profession."

"It's not that. Look. People need to die. It's how the world works. She helps people. She's got a kind heart and she feels for every subject she helps."

"So, she's going to feel really bad when she kills us?"

Max let out a long breath. "She's not going to kill us. We just need to figure this out."

"Right. Well, tomorrow I'm going to make some calls,

get in touch with my contacts and see what's being said out there."

"You mean, O'Malley's?"

Even asking the question, Max knew the truth. Fiona O'Malley was one of the top gossip mongers in the Underworld. She knew all the ins and outs of the criminal environments the way a third grader knew their way around a reading primer.

Not that the town was anything like Nocturne Falls. Far from it. No, Underworld occupied a place that was as far off the tourist track as anyone could ever get. And Fi was the queen of it all.

Or, she'd had everyone believe she was. The truth was she and Matty had had an on again off again fling that had a habit of starting out hot as a Phoenix summer and then crashing and burning like one of those solar storms on the face of the sun. Right now, however, they were ice cold in the relationship department, so Max knew how hard it must have been for his brother to decide to ask her for information.

"You don't have to do this," Max started. "I know things are tough between you two."

Matty laughed, a short, harsh, brittle sound. "Tough doesn't even begin to describe it. But, if you'd like to come along with me, I'm sure you might convince her to not cut my heart out and feed it to her dogs."

Max shrugged. It's not like he had anything else to do. Besides, he was sure Holly probably didn't want to see him right now, especially after he ditched her earlier in the evening.

"Come on. Let's go."

Without saying another word, Matty walked over to his car and climbed behind the wheel. In an odd sense of déjà vu, Max felt like he'd done this all before. Except, it had always been the other way around, with him trying to pull his brother's acorns out of the fire.

"Shut up. You're talking too much." Matty said after their riding in silence for the better part of an hour.

"I haven't said anything," Max said.

"I can hear you thinking."

Beyond tired, Max rubbed his eyes. "I don't see how this is going to help anything. I did a bad thing."

"When you were a kid."

Max sighed. "I'm pretty sure I'd reached the age of reason. I think I was around forty, by human standards, anyway."

"Like I said, practically an infant."

"As I recall, you were fighting in a war. Was it the crusades?"

Matty made a wistful sound. "Such a wonderful time. Death and pestilence, iron against flesh, and the women were so darn sweet."

"Yeah, I remember you almost getting yourself cut in half by an ax. What were you thinking? Besides, we didn't even have internet back then."

"We didn't need it. People are too informed if you ask me. Social media — nobody needs to talk that much."

Max snorted. "You are such a renaissance man."

"It was a simpler time. Believe me, brother, that was better."

"Was it? They were going to burn us at the stake a couple centuries later."

"Yes, but in my defense, I thought that being tied at the ankles and wrists and then tossed into a lake was a sort of sport. You know, like the Olympics."

Max waved his hand. "Yeah, well, we were lucky that storm happened or we both would have been spending a couple of centuries as crispy critters."

"You're so dramatic."

Finally, Matty's little sports car pulled up to the worst nightclub in a hundred-mile radius, Lucifer's Left Hand, or rather Lefty's as it was commonly referred to. Outside the front entrance was an equally disturbing sign, with blood red lettering scrawled against a solid black background. "Welcome to Underworld."

Seeing the wretched old place sent a shot of trepidation right through Max. All sorts of 'undesirables' frequented this place. Dark magic lived there as well. And, not the 'cast a spell and turn you into a toad,' stuff. No, the soul sucking, fire and brimstone sort. Rumor had it, Hell was like a summer home compared to this place.

"Let's get this over with," he said, crossing the parking lot, heading for the much smaller, much quainter establishment, O'Malley's Bar and Grille. Always in the shadows, the place could have been a mom and pop diner if it weren't for the background noise of gunfire, screaming and general chaos of its neighbor.

"I hate this place," Max said as they entered.

The dining room smelled like old shoes and the air was oppressively thick and muggy. It was because they brewed their own spirits in the back room, in addition to heaven only knew what else they cooked back there.

Still a popular place, O'Malley's had stayed in business for one principle reason. Anyone that survived the night at Lefty's usually staggered over for breakfast, and corn beef a la the prospect of surviving another day tasted pretty darned good.

"You rotten, no good, son of a..." a woman screeched across the room.

Before Max knew what was happening, the black coated Irish she-wolf launched herself through the air and landed on Matty, knocking him completely off his feet.

Then, transforming into her full, sexy woman skin, Fiona O'Malley pinned her one-time lover to the floorboards, a butcher knife against his throat and her knee in his groin.

"Hi honey," Matty said, doing his best to stretch his neck out of the way of the gleaming blade. "Long time no see."

"It's way too soon, if you ask me," she growled. "What kind of stones do you have to face me again after you dumped me for that biker-witch wannabe?"

"I admit," Matty said, squirming another two inches. "I've made some bad decisions. But, I'm a reformed man. I know when I've wronged someone and I mean to make it right."

"Oh," she said, pulling back slightly. "Like cheaters anonymous? Liar."

Max could have stood there another hour while the two worked out their problems. Unfortunately, he didn't have the time or care about whether or not they could ever make nice. He knew his brother's old girlfriend wouldn't kill him, because as bad as she talked, Fi was no murderer.

But, she could hurt him bad and then it would take forever to get the information Max so desperately needed. One thing about the she-wolf, as much as she liked hurting Matty, she loved making him all better afterwards. It was their game, after all. Heaven only knew what would happen if the two should ever grow up and actually work at a relationship. It could be epic.

"Fi," Max started, cautiously tapping on her shoulder. "I know you're upset with my boneheaded brother, but I'm in a lot of trouble right now and I could totally use your help."

As much as Fiona loved-slash-hated his brother, she'd always been very congenial toward Max. Of course, he'd never promised her the moon and then skipped out on her at sunset, either.

"Hey, Maximillian. Oh, my goodness. I didn't see you there."

Jumping up from all fours, the tall, leggy brunette was a sight to be seen. Her hair shone like midnight and her eyes were a simmering mahogany, she was as breathtaking as the stars on a clear night. Not only was she one of the most beautiful creatures on earth, she was extremely helpful in a fight. Max had once been told she bench pressed mobile homes just to stay in shape.

"Hey, Fi. How are ya?"

In answer, she pulled him into a vise-like embrace and if Max weren't a magical being, he was pretty sure she'd would have broken every bone in the trunk of his body. Fortunately, Immortals were immune to that.

"I'm as good as can be expected after having my hopes and dreams crushed by your no-good brother."

"Baby," Matty said as he climbed back to his feet. "That was almost a year ago. I'm different now. I've matured."

She sent him a scathing expression and for once Max was glad his brother backed away from it. As it was, he was kinda wishing Fiona would teach Matty about how to treat a woman.

"So," she said. "What brings you boys to my little corner of the world?"

"How about we get a table and maybe some coffee?" Max asked and Fiona warmed to him. "For you, Maxie, anything."

Ten minutes later, Max had explained his current situation and the fact that he wasn't sure whether it was all set-in motion by his own actions, or something else.

Fiona crossed her arms. "Well, I've not heard a thing about your little slip-up back in the day. I think as a new Immortal; you were probably given some leeway. After all, the guy tried to kill you and about fifty other people, right?"

Max shrugged. "True, but I thought stuff like that didn't matter. I mean, the law is the law."

"Yeah, well, mass murderers aside, evil always finds a way to take hold. Now, what I have heard is that there is a struggle going on at the High Council level."

"Really?" Max leaned closer, at the same time keeping an eye on his brother who was grinning toward one of the waitresses, a little golden minx cat woman that turned on her feline charms the minute they walked into the diner.

"Really. Same old story, and as I hear it, it's been going on awhile. A couple years back there was a big shake up. One of the top Reapers brought charges against one of the OG's, a Magical who was said to be among the first to organize things back in the day."

"Master Renault," Max said.

"I dunno. Never heard his name. Anyway, he wasn't happy and has spent half of the last century trying to figure a way back in. Then, bingo, he fell off the radar. Despite years of maneuvering to get his position back, he suddenly threw his hands up and told them 'never mind.'"

"That coincides with the order for my demise."

Fiona sat back. "Oh, wow. You're the guy?"

"The guy? What guy?"

"The unlucky one who they've been playing existential racquetball with. Word is, that if the OG gets his way, and you get Reaped, his magical powers will go off the scale. It'll be a shakeup of huge proportions."

"Wow, big brother," Matty said. "You are in huge trouble."

Max shot him a warning expression. "We are in big trouble." He turned to Fiona. "Can you keep your eyes open and let us know if anything else comes down the pike?"

"I sure can. And, for what it's worth," she said, stepping up so close that her warm breath touched him. "I'm pulling for you, Max. Him," she said, pointing to Matty. "Not so much."

Holly tried to sleep, but every time she closed her eyes, she saw Master Renault placing his long bony fingers on Max, forcing him to kneel and accept the death that he'd been given.

And, it wasn't a pretty 'close your eyes and slip into eternity' sort of death. No way.

Holly had Reaped a few Magicals that were aged in their two and three hundreds. But, none of them had been pleasant. The older the person was, especially if they still wore the face of youth, the years would come to them incredibly fast. Aging would happen within seconds and the scourge of time was not pleasant. In fact, it was horribly, terrifyingly painful. And some were said to crumple into dust.

Finally, giving up on sleeping all together, Holly climbed out of bed, grabbed her jeans and a sweater, and brushed her hair, pulling it back into a pony tail.

"Where're you going?" Artemis asked, ruffling her feathers, probably angry at having been awoken by the lights.

"Out," Holly said. Artie was her familiar, not her keeper.

"Right. Why?"

Holly let out a breath. "I need coffee."

"I'm sure there's probably some in the kitchen."

"There is, but I don't want to wake anybody up. I'm not going to get any sleep, so I might as well work."

"On what?"

"I've got my laptop. I need to do some research. So, it's

coffee and an all-night diner."

"In Nocturne Falls?"

"I already googled it. There's one only a couple of miles from here."

"Sure. Are you calling a cab?"

Holly didn't want the third degree from a bird. "No. I need to walk. Maybe it'll help clear my head."

"Be careful. You don't know what's out there."

Holly's heart softened a bit. Of course, her friend would worry about her.

"I'll be careful. But, really, who do you think is going to approach a Reaper? I'll wear my robe and cape if it makes you feel better."

"And carry the death scythe, too?"

Holly looked at her a minute. "Really?"

Artemis hissed and turned back toward the window feigning indifference. "Do what you want."

Sighing, Holly grabbed her robe and scythe and headed out the door. "See. I'm protected. I'll be back later."

What she didn't tell the bird was that she was going to stuff it in the downstairs closet. Of course, she didn't want to lug the awkward piece with her, but then, on second thought, who would be dumb enough to mess with a woman armed with a death scythe?

Exactly. So, throwing it over her shoulder, she set out for the all-night diner. The minute she exited the mansion the crisp, fall morning met her. A little chilly, it was worth it for the fresh, bracing air.

There weren't many people out this early in the morning, but a few wandered past her, and every one sent her a questionable expression. Crazy lady? Or, real Reaper, depending on whether or not she was on a mission to find her next client.

Usually, Holly carried her scythe in a case, but it would

not have been very much of a threat to any unsuspecting muggers. On the good side, she did enjoy the small amount of anonymity it afforded her. Only one guy, probably in his early twenties and carrying a skate board approached her.

"Isn't it a bit early for trick or treating?" he asked.

Holly couldn't decide if he was being a smart aleck or genuinely curious. Either way, she didn't want to engage.

"Oh, I never trick or treat," she said in a serious tone.

An expression of nervous trepidation crossed his face and he sent her a halfhearted smile. "Yeah, right. Um, see ya."

And then he crossed the street, not even near a crosswalk, to avoid any more conversing with her.

Ten minutes later she reached the diner and it smelled of fresh baked bread, bacon on the griddle and pumpkin spiced coffee. In other words, heaven.

"What can I get you?" the middle-aged waitress asked and then quickly jotted down Holly's order. Another fifteen minutes and Holly was munching on a pumpkin spice muffin and sipping a tasty chai latte. The food was a balm to her spirit even though it didn't do anything to reduce her troubles.

But, it was in that dimly lit diner that she finally could accept two very important things.

First, Max did not deserve to die. If he'd done anything in his past to warrant it, it wasn't out of a mean spirit. He may have been a bit arrogant, but that was part of his charm. And he went out of his way to be kind to others, and especially patient with Holly. Everyone made mistakes, but she was sure he just couldn't do anything that would demand his life as punishment.

The second thing Holly now admitted to was her affection for Max. Of course, it put her in a very bad position since she'd taken a vow to stay forever separate from the people who needed her services. So, no love life, no hope for marriage, no having kids and growing old with someone.

Except the more Holly was with Max, that's exactly what she wanted. And that meant only one thing.

She could no longer be a Reaper. It wasn't possible because now she'd become one of them — one of the mortals and Magics who navigated their own lives separate from any higher purpose. Oh, they had important lives and did important things, no doubt about it. But, what profession was more noble than helping someone start down the path into eternity?

And that grieved her more than anything. She was not Reaper material, and suspected she never had been. So, what was she going to do with her life now? Because even if things turned out where Max accepted his fate and gave up his life — as much as Holly didn't want him to — she would still be forever changed.

Falling in love was not acceptable for a Reaper. At least not in her guild. The moment her heart began to ache for Max was the very moment her career had ended.

And, while she was saddened to leave the most important thing she'd ever done behind, the thought of giving it all up for love did not bother her as much as it should have.

That was what had kept her up all night. Why didn't she care? Why wasn't she horrified by her disregard for the profession?

Watching the moist muffin crumble in front of her, she got a weird sense of things. It was still the same muffin, with the same flavors, the same texture, the same wonderful pumpkin smell, but it was forever different. Broken and in pieces.

And that was exactly how she felt.

Perhaps she needed to talk to someone about it. Another Reaper, maybe. A psychiatrist, might be better, but who would understand? Did they even have them for Magicals?

Her hunger receded and she sat back, sipping her tea, trying to think what she needed to do next.

Ordinarily, she'd talk to Master Renault. He more than any other Reaper had lived the longest and would surely know how best to deal with her dilemma.

And yet, she felt as if that would be a bad idea. A very bad idea. Something about her mentor left her uncomfortable, uneasy, even. Would he be sympathetic? Or, would he report her to the High Council?

It could become not only a question of her loyalties, but whether she had done anything to reduce the title of Reaper, or even illegally help a client. Or, worse yet, could she possibly have worked against the Reaper oath she'd taken?

Her life would be laid wide open and even the slightest lapse of judgement could be her undoing.

"A penny for your thoughts?"

Holly looked up to see Melody standing over her, a pumpkin coffee in one hand and an egg and cheese bagel in the other.

Letting out a breath, Holly collected herself. "Oh, you'd be wasting your money, believe me. Um, what are you doing up so early?"

The girl took the seat across from Holly. "I'm out taking an early morning run. Of course, when I ran by the diner, well, let's just say I'll be running twice as far tomorrow to work off the extra calories. Still, it's worth it."

"They do have pretty good stuff here."

Melody smiled. "Yeah, my trainer's going to be all crazy

when he finds out. And, he will. He's like FBI investigating a drug cartel. Knows everything."

Holly smiled. It was nice to chat with the young woman. Chatting was something that Reapers rarely did.

"You look troubled," the girl said, pushing her breakfast sandwich aside. "Want to talk?"

Holly hesitated. "It's probably not a good idea."

The girl waved her hand. "It's never a good idea, but sometimes you've got to. It's helps to work things out. Here. Let me start. I'm thinking you have guy troubles, and that guy happens to be my boss. Am I right?"

"Is it that obvious?"

"Sorry, but yeah. But, don't be sad. This is a great thing, right? He's so yummy, after all."

Holly let out a breath. "If I were a normal person, it would be. But, things are complicated..."

Before she knew what she was doing, Holly started to tell her everything. So much poured out of her, that once she'd started talking, the words just didn't seem to stop coming. And, to her credit, the little witch was a great listener.

"And, the worst part is, even telling you this could get me fired, or worse."

"Worse?"

"Yeah, charges brought against me, jail time..." Holly left the rest unsaid, but motioned her hand making a cutting motion across her throat.

"Ouch," Melody said. "Still, love is more important than anything. Let me do some asking around. Turns out my Aunt Matilda is very close to the HC. Let me get a line on the current board's thoughts on romance and I'll get back to you."

Holly nodded. "But, please, be careful."

"Not to worry, Reaper girl," she grinned. "I've got this."

Holly watched her swallow the last of her coffee, wink and then slip out of the restaurant. Taking a deep breath, Holly glanced down to her half empty cup of tea. It was time to get going. A shower, change of clothes, and some serious coffee would be in order.

And, who knew, maybe it would all work out, after all...

CHAPTER NINE

"AT LEAST WE GOT A little information," Max said once they were back in the car headed to Nocturne Falls.

Matty sighed like a lovesick teenager. "Yeah, but she didn't kick me out."

"She threatened to kill you, or at least hurt you really bad."

"That only means she cares."

"I'm glad she's on our side."

They drove in silence until they arrived at Nocturne Falls city limits. The sun was just beginning to come up over the horizon and the sleepy little town was waking. Just as they made it downtown, Max saw a surprising sight.

"Slow the car down. I see someone I know. In fact, just let me out at the corner. I'll walk the rest of the way home."

"Sure thing, brother. I think I'll head home, too. I could use a little sleep. And, if you hear anything, give me a call. I need to know if something's going down and there's a chance of me not waking up."

Max watched his brother pull away from the curb and once he was on his own, he turned toward the diner. He'd seen her as they pulled up to the stoplight, sitting inside the restaurant, sipping tea alone.

Taking his time, he walked into the room and suddenly became enveloped in the scents of strong coffee, pumpkin spices and cinnamon. But, he wasn't distracted by his surroundings.

"Holly?" he said, once he'd reached her table.

She'd been so intent on staring down into her cup that for a minute he didn't think she'd heard him.

Not knowing what else to do, and getting stares from the diner's other patrons, he slipped into the seat across from her.

"Hey," he said again.

She took a breath and then looked up at him. "I'm sorry," she said. "I'm afraid I'm not good company right now."

He shrugged. "For the record, neither am I. I've just spent most of the night in the car with my brother, landed in his favorite Underworld hangout and kept him from getting killed or seriously maimed by his ex-girlfriend, so I'm a little rough right now. How about you?"

"Just trying to figure things out."

"I appreciate that. Have you eaten breakfast yet? Would you like me to order you something?"

She held up her cup. "No, thanks. I've been here a couple of hours. I'm fine." She looked down for a moment. "Max, I think you should go."

"Go where? Home?"

She shook her head and he marveled at how even now, the sight of her beauty took his breath away. "No. I mean, travel. Find a place where you'll be safe."

"You mean run away."

She looked up, her eyes almost pleading him to do as she asked. "Just for a while, you know, think of it as a vacation."

"For how long? A week, a month... a century?"

He watched panic cross her expression. "I don't know. Until I get a chance to make things safe for you."

"You mean, give up my home and my business? Desert my friends and colleagues? I'm sorry. I can't do that. I won't do that."

"Then you're going to die. I don't want that."

Max crossed his arms and sat back. "I don't want that, either. But, I'm not running away, Holly. I can't"

She shook her head. "I'm not sure I can save you."

He took her hands. "I know that. Just tell me what to expect. I see you brought your, weapon." He looked over at her scythe lying on the floor beside the table.

"That's Artie's doing. She insisted I take it with me so I wouldn't get mugged along the way."

"So, what happens now? Is your boss going to show up this morning and lay hands on me or something?"

"I haven't given him my permission to Reap you. In fact, as things are, I'm the one with the power and it will remain that way unless I give it to him."

"Really? I was under the impression last night that he thinks he already has it."

She shrugged. "He does, too."

"Okay, well, back to the drawing board. How much time do we have to put him off?"

Holly shrugged. "That depends on if I can get an interview with the High Council. I'm going to put in for an audience when we get back to your place."

"That sounds promising. How long before that happens?"

"I'm hoping we get at least a week. But more than likely, it'll be three or four days."

"And Renault will be okay with that?"

She sighed. "He won't be happy, but it's my decision in the end."

Max nodded. "Well, it's a plan. How about we head back to my place, you put in your request, I'll put on a pot of pumpkin soup and we'll have a nice, relaxing day?"

"You're awfully calm about all this."

He shrugged. "Panicking won't do anything. And, if my number is going to be pulled in the next couple of days, well then, I'm going to enjoy what I can, while I can."

"Let me pay my tab and we'll get out of here."

Max held out his hand. "I already took care of it."

He stood up then and held his hand out to her. She hesitated a moment before taking it. When she did, however, he marveled at how soft and cool her fingers were, nestled in is hand. But, she had a good grip. She was petite, and very womanly, but she was also tenacious and stubborn.

Moreover, Max liked her. Everything about her. The way she smelled of sunflowers and spice. She was wild and calm and exciting and interesting. He wanted to spend eternity with her and learn every nuance of her personality. He wanted to sit up late at night and listen to her talk about whatever was fascinating her at the moment. It wasn't just a meeting of minds Max craved. He wanted to share time with her, listen to her sleeping softly, feel the warmth of her beside him.

"Are you all right?" she asked, shaking him from the depth of his thoughts. "You haven't given up, have you?"

Given up? "No," he told her. But, maybe he was surrendering to her, just a bit. "Come on. Let's get some rest."

She took his hand and smiled. "Okay."

Standing, he pulled her to her feet and delighted in the sleight weight of her. The thought of being with her flashed in his mind. Holly in his arms, in his bed, and in his life. The two of them together, arm in arm in front of a fire. Or, watching old movies on the big screen.

Looking down at her, Max realized for the first time just

what was going on inside of him. His heart beat faster, his breath came shorter, and every nerve in his body came alive. It was because somehow this woman had entered his heart. It was more than a sexual attraction, although he couldn't deny how much he wanted to be with her, there was something more, something confusing and disturbing and at the same time thrilling and exciting.

Why this woman and why him?

And yet, he somehow felt that perhaps it wasn't a mystery to be solved, but rather a moment to be savored.

Of course, one thing he knew for sure, the more he was with Holly, the more he wanted to be with her, and the more his old life teetered on the edge of oblivion.

Unfortunately, risking his life didn't bother him as much as it should have. Deep in his mind, he knew Holly was certainly worth the risk.

All the way back to the funeral home, Max and Holly walked together, hand in hand. To anyone who didn't know them, they could have been any normal couple, enjoying an early morning stroll.

But they were far from normal and every step took them closer to their destiny.

Holly couldn't help her feelings. She knew that she'd likely be ruined for what she was about to do. Though she was concerned for her own future, she was more afraid for Max. He hadn't asked for this to be thrust upon him. He'd been living his life, not hurting anyone, but still had come under the attention of the High Council.

And now, she was standing in front of him, feeling the warmth of his soul wrap around her, his very essence beckoning her forward, pulling her closer and closer.

"Holly," he said, his voice low and thick. "I want to kiss you."

There it was. This man that had collided with her in the worst possible circumstances, and all she wanted to do was accept his kiss, to melt in his arms and lose herself in him.

She swallowed. "I want you to kiss me," she barely breathed.

And, when he bent closer, he searched her eyes, and Holly knew she was truly seeing him for the first time. Not as an Immortal and not as a client, but rather as a man. It was strange for her, a woman alone. A woman who'd been traversing through life with no other thought than that of her career. There simply had been nothing — no one else in her life.

Until now.

But, there was no time to think of that. With Max so close, seconds from kissing her, and filling up all her senses, all thought left her.

The moment their lips touched, Holly experienced several things at once. The heat between them flared like kindling set ablaze after being doused with gasoline. His form was solid against her, molding around her so that they fit together perfectly. So perfectly, in fact, she knew in her soul that they belonged together.

More than that, he was kind, gentle in the way he held her. As if she were fragile glass that would shatter under the weight of a feather. Of course, she reveled in the solid firmness of him around her, enfolding her in his protective embrace. She knew he would fight monsters for her, would climb the highest mountain, or swim the deepest sea. He'd even die for her...

Holly pulled back as the shock of that thought went through her.

Gasping for breath, he looked at her, confusion and regret clouding his eyes. "What's wrong?" he asked, his voice raw.

She shook her head. "This is dangerous, you and I... like this."

He let out a breath, and then stepped back, holding his arms out wide. "Right. I don't know what I was thinking."

Suddenly it all went wrong between them. Holly felt the second it snapped and whatever they'd built had come crashing down like a house made of cards.

"I'm sorry," was all she could think to say. "It's my fault."

He shook his head. "It's not you or me. It's the situation. You're not free to be with someone. I get it. I suppose I wouldn't be good for you, either."

"I don't want it to be this way."

"Me either."

A silence fell between them in a wide and empty chasm and Holly felt that if she leaned too far toward him, she'd plummet into it.

Before she could speak again, her phone buzzed in her pocket, and without looking, she knew it was Master Renault. Of course, she'd no intention of answering him. He was going to insist that she give him the Reap and she needed strength and sleep to face him.

"I need to contact the High Council," she said, as if that would solve all her problems.

He nodded and gave her a wink. "Don't worry, Reaper girl. We'll get it figured out."

She watched him turn away and the life in the room seemed to evaporate. Her chest felt heavy and her body ached to go after him. But she stayed still, waiting until he left the room completely and closed the door behind him.

The sound of the door knob snapping into place felt like an arrow through her heart. Shaking her head, Holly pulled her phone from her jeans pocket.

Her former mentor had called her three times and on the last two the message icon was flashing.

Taking a breath, she went to her contact list and pulled up the number for Master Damon. He was her Council Liaison.

"Hello, Reaper Dent. How may I be of service?"

Holly swallowed. "I need a review of a client."

"A review? Is there a problem?'

Holly took a quick breath, "I'm having difficulties with my current assignment."

The man looked down from the picture, obviously checking his documents. "The assignment in question, an Immortal, one Maximilian Hyland. Is this correct?"

"Yes."

"And, your problem would be?"

"He's an Immortal. As in not supposed to die."

The liaison stared at her a moment. "All beings die, eventually."

That was true. Still, she had to try to save Max. "All of them? But, he's an Immortal and he's lodging a complaint. He's threatening to take legal action."

She knew it was a long shot, but even the High Council didn't like the threat of litigation lightly. There were trials that had been ongoing for centuries.

"I will submit a review. You may hold your actions until the High Council responds."

With that, the screen blanked out and Holly finally let out a breath she hadn't realized she'd been holding.

Her phone buzzed again and Holly shook her head to clear the cobwebs before answering her mentor.

"Master Renault," Holly said, trying her best to force calm into her voice.

She heard him take a breath before speaking. "Reaper Dent," he said. "I was beginning to get concerned. I've been trying to reach you all morning."

"I'm sorry. I've was unable to sleep and I went for a

walk and left my phone at home by accident."

"I see. At least you're well. Tell me, child, what troubles you?"

She'd dreaded this question from the moment she'd decided to help Max.

"I don't think Mr. Hyland should be Reaped."

There, she'd said it. She was sure she felt his expression change several times. Stunned, to angry, to disappointed. But, all of it passed in a matter of seconds. The old teacher was quick to mask his true feelings. And, if Holly hadn't been a Reaper, she might not have noticed it.

"What makes you think you have the right to speak against the High Council's wisdom?

"He's an Immortal."

"Whatever his status, it doesn't matter. He's on the list."

"I contacted the High Council, and now his Reap is on hold."

For a moment, he said nothing, but she could feel his anger simmering just under the surface. "I see. Well then, there's nothing to be done now."

Holly watched him for some sign of his ire, but this time, she saw none. "I apologize for calling you, sir. I know your time could be better spent elsewhere."

He waved his hand at her. "Nonsense. It's always good to get out into the world. And, at least now we have more time to visit."

"I'm looking forward to it, sir."

With that, his screen blacked out and Holly felt the air go out of her as well.

Exhausted from her poor sleep, her trek across town and back, and then dealing with first the High Council and then Master Renault, all she could think of was a nap.

She grasped the side rail and headed upstairs. Just a short nap and she knew she'd be back on track.

While Holly hadn't solved any of her problems, at least she'd postponed them for a while. That would have to suffice.

⤶⤷

"Of all the thick brained stunts," Renault growled as he set the phone back on the table. "She's managed to throw a wrench in it."

"What will you do?" Cravens asked.

The old Reaper walked to the window and looked out over the street. It was still morning and the October wind had picked up, shuffling leaves over the landscape. Nocturne Falls was that way. A quaint, unassuming town if you were a tourist. Stores with Halloween decorations, a bakery, a plethora of restaurants, a library, police department and so on.

The sight of it galled him. Such places were a blatant lie and he despised them. People, Magic or not, were all the same. They lived their lives without any thought for their betters.

"I think it's time we paid a visit to Mr. Hyland, ourselves."

"Do you think that's wise, Master Renault?"

"I think it's necessary. We need to know the measure of the man, learn his strengths and his weaknesses. That way, when the time comes, it will be easier to help him meet his destiny."

"Shall I fetch your coat?"

"Please." He watched his servant leave the room. Already he knew what he needed to do. And, when he was finished with the Immortal, his former student would have to be dealt with as well.

CHAPTER TEN

WHEN THE KNOCK CAME ON his office door, Max was deep in his journal. It was the war with England that had him most troubled. That was when he'd met the celebrated Daniel DeWolfe in battle. An Immortal like himself, the two had been an even match. Max fought on the side of the British, and DeWolfe under Napoleon. They'd been of equal skill and the Frenchman had fought with fury and abandon that only an Immortal could.

Or, so he'd thought at the time.

It was a very tricky thing, war. As a magical being, he couldn't hurt humans, so he had to only battle others of his kind. There were times that his human counterparts thought him a poor fighter and others they thought him a coward.

Still, when DeWolfe had called him out on that bloody battlefield, Max met him sword for sword.

Then, later, there'd been some rumor that there were Magicals who'd openly defied the law and had later been caught and executed for it.

Max thought he took every precaution. That he followed the ruling to the letter. Except, going back through his journals now, a hint of self-doubt stabbed at his mind. Was it possible his most valiant foe had not been a Mage at all? That he had been human?

And, had the High Council finally discovered his mistake? Would they be calling for his blood as well?

His thoughts were interrupted when there came a light tapping on his office door.

"Yes?"

"So sorry, sir," his housekeeper said as she peeked into the room. "But there's a gentleman here to see you. His name is Master Renault..."

Alarm shot though him and Max quickly closed the journal, but not before carefully bookmarking his place.

"Is he alone?"

The woman nodded. "Do you want me to send him away?"

Max sighed. It'd do no good to put off the inevitable. He'd do everything he could to keep from being taken. But, if he failed and these were his last moments of life, he'd regret that he wouldn't be able to say good-bye to Holly.

"Take him to the front parlor and please, make him comfortable. I'll be along directly."

The woman bobbed her head and then pulled the door closed, barely making a sound. Max found it curious, but the last few days the household and staff had been more than a little on edge. He hadn't confided in anyone but they seemed to know already.

Max checked his appearance in the mirror before leaving, meaning to show strength in the face of his adversary.

Arriving at the parlor door, Max paused a moment to study the Reaper. Though he wore the frail appearance of advanced age, the Immortal wasn't fooled. It was the way Renault's eyes darted about the room, likely measuring every surface, evaluating the amount of space in case a fight became necessary. He didn't just look around though. He rose from his seat and ran his hands along the mantle above the fireplace, where three tall candlesticks stood tall in their brass holders.

Max watched as Renault's eyes scanned the room, past the paintings that hung on each wall, to the ancient blades mounted on the far wall. Then, the hint of a smile settled on his face, barely visible beneath his long white mustache and beard. His blue eyes darkened until nearly opaque when he saw that his host waited at the door.

"Mr. Hyland," he said, bowing. "A pleasure to make your acquaintance."

Max coughed. "I wish I could say the same."

The other man's smile widened. "Oh, you think I'm here to Reap you? Oh, my heavens, that's not how it works."

Motioning for them both to sit down, Max was careful to take the seat closest to the door and farthest away from the old Reaper.

"Then why don't you tell me all about it," Max said. Reaching forward, he grasped the corner of the tea table, and while his opponent nodded and cleared his throat, Max poured himself a cup of tea.

"I'd be happy to. Of course, you know already that your fate has been determined. That being said, only my student— Excuse me, I forget that she is a fully licensed Reaper..."

"Go on," Max said.

"Of course," Master Georges said. "In order for another Reaper to do her job, she must give her consent. While it is required to be in writing, it is acceptable for her to do so verbally. That way the subject's time is not wasted."

Max almost laughed. "We wouldn't want that to happen, now would we?"

He was being sarcastic but Master Renault nodded.

"You might not believe it, but Reapers do care about their clients."

"Holly does. Do you?" He paused and waited for the other to answer him. When he did not, Max cleared his throat. "It's a simple enough question, really. Do you ever think about what you're doing, taking away loved ones, ending hopes and dreams, literally stopping time for every individual you take?

It was stealing, after all. The most precious of things, not just heartbeats, or breaths, but rather moments spent doing and being. Who among them could afford to lose time?

"Master Renault?"

Both Max and his guest turned toward the door.

Holly stood there, her green eyes staring at them both. She wore a form fitting white sweater and worn out 'skinny' jeans. Max's heart jumped at the sight of her.

Both men spoke at once.

"Holly?"

"Reaper Dent," the old man said.

Max cleared his throat. "I mean, Reaper Dent," he said, knowing that he couldn't cover his earlier impropriety.

"Master Renault, Mr. Hyland," she said, clearly uncomfortable at seeing them both together.

Both men stood.

"I hope you don't mind, dear one, but I took it upon myself to approach the subject. Of course, now that you're here, perhaps we could dispense with any further delay and proceed with the relocation process. The gentleman, as witty as he is, won't Reap himself."

Max glanced at Holly and saw her shocked expression. As soon as he did, her face colored again.

"I'm so sorry for being so inconsiderate of your rank, but I'm afraid there will be no Reaping today."

Renault made no attempt to cover his irritation. "Whatever are you talking about? And, I warn you, I may be retired, but my time is as precious as anyone else's."

Holly didn't back down and Max wanted to cheer.

"As I told you on the phone, I contacted the High Council early this morning and submitted Mr. Hyland's case for review. For the moment, his Reaping is on hold."

She might as well have openly mocked him judging by the expression he gave her.

"I see you mean to play me the fool, then."

She stepped forward. "I assure you, that was not my intention. I take full responsibility for your inconvenience. I will, of course, cover your expenses and make notification to the High Council of how you came to my aid. Your effort won't go unnoticed, I assure you."

Max was fascinated by the strength exuded by the woman in front of him. Though she was clearly a foot and a half shorter than her counterpart, there was no difference in their stature.

In response, the old Reaper took a menacing step forward, but Max slipped in front of Holly.

"I beg you sir," he said in a tone that was not at all requesting. "To think about what you are doing. I might not be an all-powerful Reaper, but I've wielded many a sword. As a Mage, you and I are equal in the eyes of the law. And, though I believe you aren't as frail as you make yourself appear, I know I'm in pretty good condition when it comes to athletic acumen."

That clearly gave the old master a reason to pause. He bowed again. "Of course, I apologize for my behavior. It looks as though I'm but an old fool, after all."

"Nonsense, sir. You are clearly acting in accordance with our order."

Max disagreed, but kept his own council. "If you would

like, sir, I can summon my cook to prepare a meal. It would be an honor to have you at my table."

The old man waved a hand. "Nonsense. It's clear the two of you have formed a... friendship. Since your time left is limited, well more so than I originally thought, I leave the two of you to your, ahem, enjoyments. If I were you, I'd make every minute count."

Standing at the parlor window, Holly watched her former mentor climb into the rental car and then drive away. As soon as the red Prius turned the corner and was gone from sight, she let out her breath.

She'd done her best to put on a brave face, but now her insides turned to jelly.

"Nice fellow," Max said behind her. "I can't wait until he visits again."

Holly spun around, a combination of anger, fear and relief mixing in her gut. "What were you thinking, confronting him without me present?"

Max shrugged. "He seemed harmless enough."

"Is that what you think? He's slain entire armies."

"Has he? I thought Reapers were all peace-loving Magical beings. High and mighty Mages, who wouldn't dream of playing with our lives like we were nothing more than toys." He leaned forward and pulled her into his arms. "Want to go play a round of Reap the Immortal? I hear it's all the rage."

"Quit mocking me," Holly said, though his estimation was pretty close to the truth. "I'm not sure how much time we have. The Council could make their decision a week from now or tomorrow. There's no predicting what political machinations are stirring within their ranks."

"What do we do?"

Holly let out a breath. "We need to go back to your

journals, I think. Surely, the answers will be in there."

She started to turn away, but Max put his hand on her arm. His touch was much as she remembered, warm, firm, and promising so much more.

But there wasn't time to think of that now. Too much was at stake.

"What is it?" she asked, sensing a change in his mood.

"I think I found out why my name was selected for Reaping."

His tone was no longer one of playful romance, nor was it his usual staunch, serious tone. It was different. Darker.

And, it scared the devil out of her.

"You found something."

He nodded and looked away, shame coloring his expression. "You've heard of the term, 'imposters' haven't you?"

Holly shrugged. It didn't sound all that bad. "People pretending to be other people. So, what?"

His head still downcast, she could feel his gaze slide upward only to look away again. "Whether in jest, or even as a fraud, that pretty much sums it up. Except when it comes to Immortals."

"Explain."

He motioned her to sit with him on the sofa and fear started to stir in her stomach. When she was settled, he sat down beside her and took her hand.

"For a time, most of mankind knew about the magical races. Although, some still believe to this day, most think magic is a joke or a fantasy. In those days, it was a great thing to be a member of a magical race. We were revered, much like rock stars are today. There were those who aspired to be Magics, even though they weren't born to it."

"I don't like where this is going," Holly said, her throat suddenly dry.

"It was a more barbaric time. But, the laws were the same. Mages, Immortals weren't allowed to harm humans, Magics, or even other Immortals. Very clear on that."

She knew the rules about injuring — or even killing — humans, but wasn't sure where he was going with this. "Tell me," she said at last.

Max cleared his throat again. "It was war..."

"It always is." Realizing she wasn't helping anything, she coughed. "I'll be quiet. Please, continue."

He sighed. "I was in Wellington's army, fighting the French in Spain. I tried to remain out of the main battle, you know. I worked the ambulances, carrying to fallen from the field."

"A good choice for an Immortal."

He grinned. "I thought so. Anyway, after carrying more than twenty men, some injured, some dead, I'm sorry to say, I happened upon a French officer who'd been lying beside a dead horse. He'd become tangled in the animal's tack, and had one leg wedged beneath the beast. Being a kind sort, I stopped to help him. After pulling him from his saddle, I did my best to give first aid."

"Didn't you realize he was an enemy soldier?"

Max nodded. "I did. But, I made it a policy to not differentiate between the fallen. It was the humane thing to do."

"It was."

He warmed toward her and Holly soaked it up like a sunflower facing the dawn.

"Anyway, the soldier jumped me when I wasn't looking. I tried to stop him, thinking he'd awakened disoriented, but he confessed that he'd been lying in wait, meaning to ambush me instead. He pronounced himself an Immortal as well and accused me of being a traitor to my kind."

"He wasn't an Immortal?"

Max shook his head. "I was so sure he was. I mean, he fought like no human I've ever seen. Several times he cut me with his bayonet, and twice he pinned me down. I almost didn't escape with my body intact. In the end, I bested him. Thinking he was only unconscious, I left him lying there, in what I thought was the reparation sleep. When I was going over my entry this morning, I did a full memory retrieval and sure enough, I'd been so messed up myself, I hadn't even seen it."

"The High Council missed it, too."

"They must have been doing some critical information searches and found out what happened."

"Or, you were betrayed."

"By who?"

She looked at him then, and as realization dawned on them both, she wished a lightning bolt would strike her where she sat. Anything rather than speak the truth of it.

But, she couldn't hold it back.

"By someone who was there."

"My brother."

CHAPTER ELEVEN

IF IT HADN'T BEEN FOR Holly's presence, Max knew he would have lost it. Even though it had been her arrival that had begun his descent into this insanity, it was she who'd become the anchor against the storm that threatened to overtake him.

What stood in the face of it all was that he'd been betrayed — and by his own brother?

"A part of me wants to deny it all, of course. But, I know my brother."

"Why would he do such a thing?" she asked, concern darkening her expression. "I mean, he is family, after all."

Max shrugged. "It's not in his nature to do such a thing, unless he's backed into a corner. But, then again, his mortality is tied to mine."

"Then, he's not suspect?"

Max thought for a moment. "It wouldn't be the first time he's created a problem and then waited for me to fix it."

"What are you going to do?"

He shrugged. "Nothing. He's my brother and I won't lift my hand against him."

"That's very noble of you," she said, crossing her arms.

He leaned closer, catching the hint of jasmine and vanilla from her hair. "I take it you're an only child?"

She shot him a sharp expression. "I am. Why?"

"Because you don't understand siblings. You always love them, sometimes hate them, often are disappointed or furious with them, but you never give up on them."

"I suppose it's even more so since the two of you are twins?"

"Matty is my best friend and my worst enemy."

Standing up, she began to pace. A part of him was upset at losing her closeness, but another part enjoyed watching her. It was these unguarded moments that he liked her the best. Concentrating on the way she moved, each step as precise as a dancer, he knew she could take flight at a moment notice, or stand steadfast in a fight.

But, it wasn't just that. He'd watched how she interacted with people. Hers was a touch of firm support and gentle guidance. Which made her perfect for a Reaper, he thought ruefully.

What would happen if she lost her status because of him? Surely, those traits were necessary for other professions?

"What would you do if you could no longer be a Reaper?"

The question caught her cold. "I haven't given it much thought."

"I'm just saying, with all that's happening, perhaps you should."

She watched him a moment, at first her expression darkened with suspicion as she was trying to figure him out. But, then, a more thoughtful, unguarded look crossed her features.

"Help people," she said as though the idea was still forming in her mind. "I guess..."

"Because that's what you do now. You don't want to create art or build bridges, or even open a bed and breakfast? Nocturne Falls is the perfect place for it, you know."

He watched as his words struck her and she did all but duck from them. "As for creating anything artful, I can't draw a straight line, I'm tone deaf, and there's a reason I wear mostly black."

"Okay, no art. I suppose that lets out building bridges?"

"I can't make wooden blocks stand up." She crossed her arms, daring him to speak otherwise.

"Hospitality?"

"Do I look like I have the patience for hospitality?"

Looking at her at that moment, her green eyes blazing and her copper hair flying in all directions did not lend to a 'come and sit a spell' hostess.

"Fine. Let's see what your strong qualities are, then."

"Why do you care?"

"Because I do. Except for my chaotic relationship with my brother, I have no one that cares about me. If I'm correct, neither do you. I know how that feels and no one should ever be so alone."

That seemed to send a shock wave right through her. She batted her eyelashes, and he guessed by the way she appeared to try to speak but no sound came out, there was a juggernaut of words stuck inside her.

"Oh," she said at last, turning away from him. "I'm very sympathetic."

"Empathetic," he corrected. Touching her shoulder, he turned her back to face him. "I can see that you often feel the pain of those in your care."

"I do."

"And you put everyone before yourself, always."

She bit her lip. "What are you up to?"

He shrugged. "Just stating the facts."

"Right. And, what about you?"

Well, that was a question he wasn't expecting. "What

about me? I own a funeral home. It's what I do."

"I find it odd that you, a man who is supposed to live forever, would choose a career dealing with death."

"I see what you're doing here. That's a bit uncomfortable, now isn't it?" He waited a second to let the comment pass, but it did not. "Fine. Even for an Immortal, life is not guaranteed. Not dying doesn't include not suffering or not succumbing to depression, anxiety, or pain. It just means you stay alive."

"Forever," she said, a tinge of emotion in her voice.

"Forever. Believe me, it's not all it's cracked up to be. You can get tired of living. Especially when people all around you die — over and over again."

He hadn't meant to have that wistful sound in his voice. He waved her off. "I don't want sympathy, believe me. I know how lucky I am. And, there's my brother. A lot of Immortals don't have family so it's very rare for there to be twins."

The Reaper let out a breath. "Look at us. We have it all but we're both miserable."

That made him chuckle. "Too right. Which brings us back to my problem. What the blazes am I going to do?"

"For one, you're going to let me help you."

He held up his hand. "I don't think so. It's too risky for you to get involved. I'll take on the High Council myself. No need for both of us to go down if we can prevent it."

Suddenly, her emerald eyes grew almost opaque and a red tint lighted her cheeks and the tips of her ears. "You've no need to worry about me. I can hold my own against the High Council, and Master Renault, too. I've been wronged as much as you."

"Oh really?"

She stepped forward so that they were practically nose to nose, well, nose to chest. Chin tilted upward, her eyes burning right through is self-sacrificial expression.

"I was set up to fail. Somebody wants me ruined or possibly even prosecuted. I don't know why, but it's true."

"Do you think so?"

"I do. And, I mean to find out who it is."

He let out a breath.

It was a dangerous path for an Immortal, but then again, what was the point of living forever if you didn't enjoy any of it? He was a good man. He'd helped many, been a good friend and a fierce warrior. More than that, he'd lived a good life. Didn't he deserve happiness, too?

"No matter how this ends, if I can, I'll help you figure it out."

He meant it, too. For, what was a life where no risks were taken?

Very simple.

Death.

⌘

"This is unacceptable!" Master Renault stood white-faced in front of the High Council. "The subject has a clear order for assisted passage. Why is this not being dealt with?"

The three council members present looked from one to another. One was tall and thin with hair that was the color of spun silver that went down his shoulders to the floor. He was clean shaven with cerulean blue eyes that sparkled like diamonds. The second was shorter, with dark hair cropped close and he wore a beard and mustache trimmed to perfection, his eyes were the shifting colors of hazel and green. And the third was a woman, with thick strawberry blond hair that gathered in waves around her head and floated like angelic feathers. But her eyes were as black as onyx and her skin pale as porcelain.

"What is your complaint, Georges?"

Renault bristled at the lack of respect they showed him.

"There is a clear order to Reap this man. I demand to know why it's not being done."

The woman, tilted her head to the side. "And this is your concern, why?"

"A former student of mine contacted me for guidance when he resisted her attempts to take him. I'm a highly-decorated Reaper with centuries of experience..."

"Who has been retired for decades."

"Not by choice," he ground out. "I've stayed away. Remained in exile, as I've been ordered."

The tallest one nodded. "Not exile," he said. "Retirement. You were given a generous retirement package. You should be content with that. You've the entire world to do with as you please."

"What pleased me was doing my job. But, I'm not here to argue that. I'm only here to assist my former student."

The councilman who'd remained silent the entire time cleared his throat. "The matter of the Reaping of Maximillian Hyland is under review. A complaint has been lodged and before we can allow the Reaping to continue we must make sure we have given it every consideration."

"How long will that be?"

The woman sighed. "We cannot predict that. Unless the subject relinquishes his inquiry and submits to the Reaping, we cannot proceed. Presently, the Reap is on hold."

The screen went blank. "Typical, bureaucrats," he spat. It was clear that he was going to get no help from them. He would have to convince Holly to give him the Immortal's Reap.

"Any luck?" his servant asked. He was carrying in a tray with a cup of tea, steaming and filling the room with an aroma of cinnamon.

"No chance that the damn council will knuckle under.

No, I'm going to have to go after Holly. Trouble is, she's not the weak-willed ninny that she once was. Stood up to me as if I were the underling and she the master."

"What will you do?"

"Convince her that the Immortal is not who or what she thinks. He's a killer."

"How will you do that?"

He smiled for the first time since he'd been tossed from the funeral home. "By showing her the truth, that's how. Once she learns how despicable he is and how he needs to be put down, she'll have to understand."

"She will?"

"Yes. Even if she doesn't, it's of little matter. He's too strong for someone at her level. She must give him to me. And, when she does, it won't be an easy time for him. I'm going to make sure of that."

"If anyone can, it's you, Master Renault."

"I've a list of things I need you to do. When you've finished, come back here and I'll set things in motion. Now, I've some calls to make."

No matter what the High Council commanded, nor what Reaper Dent had to say about it, he would take the Immortal down and when everyone knew what he'd done, the power would be his. No one would be able to deny him his place on the Council. Once all was done, he would make them pay for how they'd treated him. From his former student, to the soon to be former High Council.

They would regret how they'd treated him to their very last breaths. He would make sure of it.

CHAPTER TWELVE

HOLLY WATCHED MAX WORK THROUGH the last of his journal. "I need to go through some things," she told him. "I'll be upstairs. When you finish what you're doing, perhaps we could order in?"

He looked up from his book. "Of course. I've got two more volumes to get through and then we can decide what we want for dinner."

Just then a knock sounded at the door and Max's assistant poked her head in.

"Hey boss, Mac Lemore and his are here for their appointment."

He let out a breath. "I'm sorry. I must go see to them. They're planning their uncle Joe's funeral."

"Oh, has he passed away recently?" She wondered if she could have been any help to the family.

"No, not yet. Though to hear him tell it, he's been dying for the last five years. But, he wants to make sure everything is to his exact specification."

"A little controlling, is he?"

Max grinned. "He's been running his family since he was a boy in short pants. He wants to run everything, including where I order the flowers from and how I set up the itinerary at the gravesite."

"Is he a Magical?"

"No, but I wish he was. I could go another five hundred years before I bury him. He's kind of a swell guy."

"Sounds like it." She sighed. "That's it, funeral guy. I'm out of here. I need to go to the library and do some digging in the law archives. With any luck, we can find a loophole to get us out of this mess."

He grinned and watched her leave.

Of course, he knew there were no loopholes. When it came to the High Council and the Immortals, they never gave in. After all, he hadn't been the only Immortal ever to screw up. Still, there was no harm in her trying, either.

As it was, he did have something to do and he definitely didn't want Holly involved. It was time to get the truth out of the one person he now knew was involved. And, if it involved a little butt kicking to get it done, well, he was all for that.

He plucked his phone from his pocket.

"Hey, Melody. Thanks for the diversion. I needed a little alone time."

"Sure thing boss. Anytime you want me to lie, I'm your girl."

"That's an uncomfortable thought. And, you did agree to it rather quickly." He couldn't help wondering if there was anything else his assistant had lied to him about.

He heard her laugh as she clicked off the phone.

As if fate had taken a hand, his phone rang immediately and he saw a familiar name pop up.

"Hey, brother. Just the guy I wanted to talk to."

"Great, Maxi. Because I've got a whole lotta info for you." He laughed. "And boy are you going to be surprised. Stuff is going on, brother dear. You're not going to believe the half of it."

Max heard the click of his brother hanging up the call. Of course, he didn't want his brother to be a deceitful liar.

He remembered when they were boys during the middle ages and their mother rescued them from the Inquisition, virtually pulling them from the fire.

Even today, he could still smell the smoke, hear the crackling of the wood piled around the two of them.

Sadly, his mother didn't manage to escape. Having never known their father's identity, Max and Matty had been given to the care of an elderly woman who'd been his mother's maid back when she'd been living as a consort to a wealthy landowner.

Growing into men, the two had had long discussions about their father. All their mother had told them was that their sire had been a very powerful warlock and that before the boys had been born, he'd discovered their immortality.

At the time, it had been considered a blessing and a curse, but now Max suspected it was more a result of a genetic mutation rather than Magic. He'd learned that much during his scientific phase, which had led him to become a funeral director.

Sighing, he got up from his desk and carefully put his journals way, turning the key in the library's lock, and made his way downstairs. Holly wouldn't be gone long and he'd much to do. Because their future was so uncertain, he wanted to spend as much time with her as possible.

"Shall I start dinner, Mr. Max?" Cook asked him as he reached for the front door handle.

"I'm not sure when I'll be home. Just make sure there's something quick and easy. Soup and sandwiches, maybe. Or, perhaps some stew that even I can heat up. Or, whatever Ms. Dent would like, but nothing elaborate."

"Yes, sir." The older woman sighed. A great grandmother, the servant loved treating him like one of her grandchildren — who had grown and moved away.

Now, to see to his brother. All the way he recited his usual litany of reasons he shouldn't beat the living daylights out of his twin.

It would have been all too easy to take his frustrations out on Matty.

But, Max was no longer fighting battles with his fist or his sword. Not even with more modern weapons that were now so easily available.

He fought only with words these days and lucky for him, over the years he'd become quite adept.

And of course, when it came to his twin, in a battle of wits, Matty was generally unarmed. Which was a good thing, because if he'd been any other way, Max might not have been able to resist at least punching him in the nose.

Max still owed him one from the last time when Matty had given a traffic cop Max's name to avoid a 'driving while impaired' ticket. When the police came knocking on his door with the arrest warrant after Matty failed to appear in court, it was clear he was not the same man, but they still had to take him in and he'd had to prove that he wasn't the guy they'd taken into custody that night.

Well, maybe he deserved one punch...

❧

"This is an unexpected visit, Master Renault," the short, round man said. He looked around furtively. "This is dangerous, us meeting like this."

Renault slid into the booth across from one of the High Council's oldest sitting Council members. Master Marcus Roundel wiped his damp brow with a trembling hand.

"Things have changed, and you well know it. Besides, it's so dim in here one would have to be an owl to identify me. I've read the room. No one here cares about us."

They were seated in Mage's Bar, catering to the more 'magical' of palates. The place had a virtual witch's brew of delights for spirits.

"What is it you want?"

Renault considered the desperate man in front of him. Short, round, balding, possessing the second highest position of the Reaper's guild though he looked more like an accountant than a powerful Mage.

"The Council's not going to back my play."

The other man waved his hand. "Of course they are, you fool. It'll just take some time."

"Time? How much time? I'm tired of rotting away in the frozen north while you all sit on your laurels arguing what to do with the Immortal."

Roundel licked his lips. "There was a complaint made, by your own underling, by the way."

"Granted, she was not as malleable as I thought. Definitely a disappointment, that one."

"Right. Well, now we have to take our time. After the Benson affair, the councilors are very hesitant to make a rash decision. I mean, it all looks good on the surface, sure, but what if there were extenuating circumstances?"

"Extenuating circumstances? You are part of the most powerful organization in the entire realm of magic and you're sniveling in fear, telling me you're worried about a little lawsuit?"

"You don't understand. It's not like the old days. We're under so much public scrutiny these days."

Renault had had enough. He slammed his fist on the table. "We had an agreement, you spineless weasel. I help you put away your counterparts and give you full lead of the High Council and you bring me out of retirement. Has that changed?"

Roundel paled. "No. Of course, not. It's just that we'll have to find another way. Sacrificing the Immortal isn't going to be enough. You'll have to come up with another plan."

"I see," Georges ground out. "It's to be that way, is it?"

The other man spread out his hands in front of him. "I understand your frustration. Believe me, I share in it. I wish there was more I could do."

Georges crossed his arms. He'd had his doubts about his reluctant partner's abilities. He'd withered at the first hint of trouble.

Very well then, he thought. "Not to worry," he told Roundel. "I'll manage it." Finishing the last of his drink, Renault stood up.

Roundel let out a nervous breath. "Excellent. What are you thinking?"

"I'd rather not say right now. I need to flush it out a bit first. Good day."

With that, he left his former accomplice to finish his drink.

He waved to his servant as he got into the cab. "Plans have changed."

"Master Renault?"

"I'm not going to just come out of retirement. I'm going to rid our guild of those weak-willed ninnies we call a High Council and take control of it myself."

"Heads are gonna roll, are they?"

"They are indeed," Renault said. "I'm going to end them, once and for all."

CHAPTER THIRTEEN

"WHAT'S THE MATTER, MAX? YOU don't have what it takes to put me down?"

Max stood stone still, staring at his twin. He very much did have what it took, and then some. But, once again, he had to ask himself, to what purpose?

Other than maximum enjoyment, that was.

The two were standing practically nose to nose in the main living space of the small cottage that Matty rented. A typical 'bachelor's pad' it was basically one large room, with a walk-in closet on one side and a half bath on the other. Between the two was a small kitchen and directly across from that was the front door. The rest of the place was crowded with an oak table and chairs on one side and a three-piece leather sofa set. Dominating the far wall was a sixty-inch flat screen television that hung above a faux fireplace. Of course, the decor was completed by Matty's clothing strewn about the room, draping all the furniture and most of the floor. The final touch was a sink full of dirty dishes that, judging by the odor that emanated from the kitchen, had been forgotten for some time.

"I don't want to put you down, Matty. You're not a dog and I'm not the bad guy here. You betrayed me. I want to know why."

That seemed to set him back. Suddenly he paled and his

eyes widened. "What are you accusing me of, exactly?"

By the tone of his brother's voice, Max realized that Matty wasn't as vigorous as he should have been for his own defense.

"I think you know," he said, crossing his arms. If the situation did escalate, he was more than willing to go back to his boxer's pose. "But, in case you need reminding, somebody alerted the High Council to my involvement with a certain French officer."

If Matty was pale before, now he was practically translucent.

"Yeah," he gulped in a deep breath. "About that. It wasn't intentional."

"Not intentional? three centuries later and I'm being Reaped because of it and it wasn't intentional? What, you tripped and accidentally told them all about my past?"

"You don't understand," Matty said. "They had me cornered."

"Who?"

He rubbed his eyes. "It's better if I don't say. I got into a little financial tangle and needed some fast cash, um, and then when I couldn't pay them back..."

"With whom did you get into a 'little tangle'?"

Matty crossed his arms over his abdomen and looked down at his feet. "The Wharton clan."

Max stepped back, suddenly understanding his brother's desperation. The Whartons were a powerful family of warlocks who operated one of the biggest organized crime businesses this side of the Atlantic. Gambling, racketeering, and corruption, they'd been on the major watch lists for years. It was said one of their founding members was the nephew by marriage to a member of the High Council, Master Roundel.

No wonder his brother sold him out. It wasn't just a

few broken bones he faced, but torture of a different sort — being labeled as an enemy to the Whartons made you open season to any half-Magic cowboy out there. They were known to run competitions on who could inflict the most damage before the kill. Worse than that, they didn't just stop at the perpetrator. Everyone he'd ever known, befriended, and even loved became targets too.

"They took payment in another form."

"Evidently, Master Roundel paid your debt."

He shrugged. "Most of it. Anyway, it's nothing for you to worry about. Well, except for the Reaper thing."

"They're going to take me unless I can figure out a way to earn a full pardon."

"If anybody can get one, it'll be you, brother." Matty held out his hands. "They already overlooked it once."

"I don't even know why they let it pass the first time. He was a human and I killed him. End of story."

"It was a mistake. There was no way you could have known he wasn't an Immortal."

"They've never made mention of it in all this time. I assumed that my case was dismissed."

"Maybe you can ask them?"

As simple of an idea as it was, Max thought perhaps the direct approach was the best. "You mean request an audience."

"It can't hurt, can it?"

Matty sighed. "At worst I'll be detained until the judgement comes down. If I'm found guilty and they choose to end me, that means there'll be no escaping for either of us."

Matty nodded. "It's a risk, true enough, but this won't go away. Your best shot is to confront them."

"How did you become so wise, little brother?"

Matty shrugged. "Like it or not, I think you're rubbing

off on me. Never thought that would happen."

Max chuckled. "I'll ask them to spare you. I'm not sure if it's possible, but I suppose it won't hurt to ask."

"I agree, but I appreciate the sentiment, just the same."

Max spread out his hands. "It's the least I can do."

Matty walked over to his brother and grasped his shoulder. "Hey. If anybody can get us out of this alive, it's you."

"Why?"

Matty chuckled. "Because, that's what you do, Maxi. It's just what you do."

"You make it sound like fate."

Matty shrugged. "Fate-schmate. It's who we are. I screw things up and you fix 'em, big brother."

"Since you've fulfilled your part of the bargain, it looks like it's my turn to step up."

With that, he turned around and left the cottage. Before he 'turned himself in,' Max had a few things to take care of first. Papers had to be filed and notices had to be sent — just in case things went south.

Max looked in his rear-view mirror once as he pulled away from the house. His twin had followed him outside and now watched him leave.

A sobering thought occurred to him. It might very well be the last time he ever saw his brother on this side of the veil.

⌗

The car was an older model Cadillac sedan but it had a smooth ride. It was a bright red, two-door dream to drive, and though she'd not done much driving since becoming a Reaper, Holly did enjoy it. Something about cruising around town made her feel carefree and light hearted.

She'd gone a long time without feeling anything but sadness.

"That's no way to live," she said and was surprised at the

tone of regret in her voice. The next thing she knew, tears started to flow and she was sobbing like she'd just lost her best friend. "What's wrong with me?"

She gave in to the torrent of tears. It wasn't altogether sadness she felt, though. Thankfully, there was joy in the mix as well. For the feeling of freedom she felt and for the beginnings of hope for a future.

Things with Max were still up in the air, of course. And, if anything happened to him, she would be crushed. Her feelings were so new and raw where he was concerned, she knew she'd never get over his loss.

Which made her even more desperate to get things settled. So, that left only one thing to do.

She had to confront her former mentor once and for all.

Twenty minutes later she was parked in the Harbor Inn Hotel parking lot. Spanish style, the long lazy design of it with arching doorways made it look like it belonged in another time, another world. It should have been set under tall pine trees covered with low hanging moss. She'd called the hotel earlier and found out which room Master Renault occupied. Time to get her meeting over with.

Climbing out of the car, she'd no more than set both feet on the ground when she saw his room's door open and him walking through it.

Her stomach tightened. As a novice Reaper, she'd literally feared him. Even as time went on, her reaction to him had lessened, but there was always that edge in her gut when she knew they would cross purposes.

"Master," she said, nodding respectfully.

His face remained expressionless, arms folded into his royal blue robe. It was a startling contrast to the simple attire he'd worn earlier that day. Although no longer a High Reaper, and he owned his ruling garments, by law he was not allowed to appear in public in them unless he'd gotten special permission. And, that was rarely, if ever given.

Basically, once you were out of the guild, you were out of the guild.

"Reaper Dent." He barely bobbed his head which was an insult, really. Despite his retired status, as an active Reaper, she was now his superior.

Holly decided to let it pass. He could spit on her for all she cared, as long as Max was released from his contract.

"We need to talk," she said, ignoring the inadequacy of her words. "What the Council is doing is wrong. What you're doing is wrong."

He smiled then, a thin red line that cut through is face. "On that, we don't agree. Since you're so eager to persuade me to change my mind, it would be best not to have our 'discussion' where others might hear it. My room, perhaps?"

Glancing quickly to the hotel, Holly became aware of two things. First, that going into his hotel room was completely inappropriate and second, who knew what tricks he would be able to pull on her once he had her secluded in there?

"I think not," she said, clenching her jaw, doing her best to clamp down her anxiety.

"You don't trust me. Very well, there is a nice little park behind the hotel. Perhaps we could talk there?"

Holly hesitated. Was it possible he had something else planned for her? She started to refuse but he held is hand up.

"You've no need to worry. We're alone and it's a straight run back to your rental. And, well, look at me. It's not like I could catch you if you ran away."

She knew that was a lie. He wore his old man persona as

a disguise. Also, his magic was unaffected by his age. While Reapers didn't have the magic of Witches and Warlocks, they had several spells at their disposal. If he wanted to he could attempt a paralysis spell, or a stumbling spell, or even a sleeping spell.

Of course, Holly was a Reaper, too. Whatever he could throw at her, she was younger and faster. Girding her strength, she nodded.

"The park is fine."

He held out his hand to her, but Holly didn't take it. She knew his gesture wasn't genuine.

It was a nice, shaded area with a playground off to one side and a small goldfish pond on the other side. There was a cleanness in the air and when Holly breathed it, she smelled a mixture of baking apples and cinnamon nearby.

"Quite a lovely little place," Master Renault said as he motioned her to take a seat across from him at one of the picnic tables.

"It'll do for our purposes."

Keep it professional, she told herself. *Stay firm and don't let him get ahead of you.* Shoulders back, she followed him to the table. Taking long strides, she walked past him without sparing him so much as a glance.

One thing she knew for sure was that seeing him here now could only mean that he'd interests in Max's Reaping, and why that was, she'd no idea.

What could he possibly gain from Max's death?

Was it possible that he had engineered this entire situation?

Taking a seat with her back to the sun, she crossed her arms and waited. He approached her slowly, arms at his side, wearing an expression of controlled calm. In all the years she'd known him, she'd seen the same expression, no matter the difficulty of the Reaping, no matter the deluge of orders that came down. He met her gaze, without so much as blinking.

For a moment, she thought he might remain standing. In the back of her mind she remembered others that had looked down on her as well. Parents. Teachers. Bullies. It was a position of power. Very well, she wasn't that impressionable young girl who'd been under his tutelage any more.

She began to stand up, but he held out his hand and then slowly descended onto the bench.

"You'll have to excuse me. My old joints don't work as well as they once did."

Holly eased back to her seat. "What do you want?" she asked.

Judging by the way he blinked, her direct question surprised him. But he recovered quickly. "I want what's rightfully mine, like anyone."

"Yours?"

"Mine." He let out a breath. "I wasn't ready to retire. I have so much left to do."

It was at that moment that Holly heard something sinister in his tone, noble birthright and entitlement. For the first time, she realized that the man she'd known and trusted all those years was not at all who she'd thought he was.

"So, to reverse your status, you decided to take the life of an Immortal and pull me into the process as well?"

Her mentor shrugged. "It's not like you could have done the job yourself. And, the Immortal? Paha! He was living on borrowed time as it was. Sooner or later someone was going to discover the oversight."

"Oversight? This is a man's life we're talking about." The blood in her veins turned to ice. She'd heard of other Reaper guilds that had been invaded by corruption and had been dealt with accordingly.

"And you included me in this."

He waved his hand at her. "I knew you'd never be able to complete the job."

Anger stirred in her gut. Not because he was so presumptuous but because he was right. She was a mid-level Reaper at best. Still, she'd worked hard and done as good a job as she could have.

"Never mind that," she said. "To take a man's life so carelessly... How could you?"

He gave her a puzzled look. "It's what we do? Have I mentored you so poorly, that you don't understand what our life's work is? We are Reapers. We take lives."

"We help people."

"We guide the living onto the ethereal plane, into eternity. That's all. We don't befriend them. We don't sympathize with them. We are soul collectors for our guild and nothing more."

"You're wrong," she started to say, but realized that her words would have no effect whatsoever.

His smile softened and he reached across the table and patted her hand. "Do you know what your problem is? You're in the wrong profession. You want to heal people? You want to ease their pain? Then go to medical school."

The anger in Holly's gut whirled into cold fury. His words resonated with her somehow, but then, she knew it could be his Reaping power had increased somehow. His magic had taken another turn and it wasn't all the puppies and kittens type of magic. In fact, when she calmed her nerves, let her senses focus on his underlying vibes, she felt it. Something rotten. Something evil. Something heinous and detestable.

And he'd no regard for her life or anyone else's.

He had to be stopped and she had no idea how to do it.

CHAPTER FOURTEEN

BACK AT HOME, MAX WAITED anxiously on Holly's return. As the hour grew later and later, afternoon slipped into evening and there was no sign of her.

He stood at the window, gazing out into the evening.

"Need anything before I head home?" Melody asked as she pulled on her jacket. "I finished up the last of the invoices and rescheduled the urn deliveries."

"No, thanks. I'm good."

Melody hesitated at the door. "Boss, what's really going on?"

He sent her a guarded expression. "What do you mean?"

"You're spending a lot of time with the Reaper lady. Something serious?"

Max let out a breath. "You could say that."

"Then why aren't you happier?"

Happiness. That was a term that Max had never tried to get too close to. Living a long time didn't necessarily mean that one enjoyed all the centuries he was forced to inhabit. It wasn't the sadness of one lifetime, but of many.

He spread out his hands. "I'm happy enough, I guess. At the moment, I'm enjoying Reaper Dent's company. No matter how things turn out, she's been a gift."

Melody tilted her head to one side. "I'm glad of that,

boss. You deserve happiness, you know. You're not a bad guy."

He smiled and nodded. "One would think so."

Max wanted to say more, to explain that he'd not had an easy life, that despite his immortality, he'd pretty much screwed up a lot of it. But, how does one explain oneself to someone who hasn't experienced what it was like to be him?

Even his twin didn't really understand. After all, Matty hadn't been as serious in his pursuits. He hadn't been all about justice and fighting for causes he didn't belong to.

All the same, Melody gave him a reassuring pat on the shoulder. "You worry too much, boss. That girl is crazy about you. Trust me, witches know all about these things."

She winked and sauntered out of the room.

Just then he saw a strange car pull up in the drive. To his surprise, Holly jumped out of the driver's side and ran toward the house.

Something was bad. Very bad.

Heading for the front door, he ran into Mel and just barely missed knocking her over. The door swung open and Holly burst through.

"Get your gear," she called out as she ran for the stairs. "We've got to get out of here now."

"What?" both Max and Mel said.

But, she was already halfway up the stairs. "No time to explain! He's coming!"

Mel recovered before he did. "Did you hear what she said? Move. I'll cover you both as long as I can."

Max had seen Mel do her witch thing, and as far as such things went, she was an impressive spell caster, but he doubted she was any match for what they were up against.

"Right. He ran to his office, unlocked his desk drawer and pulled out the only thing of value that he owned. It might not seem like much, but the old talisman had been his mother's and he'd always kept it with him. Of course, Matty had one just like it, in case anything happened to him, but still, the thought of not having at least a small piece of her close to him made him feel terribly vulnerable and extremely sad.

"Max?" Holly called out. "Where are you?"

"Here," he called back, slamming the drawer shut and locking it. Everything else he owned could be replaced. He'd been smart with his investments, and had at least a dozen accounts he could draw from if needed.

Running out of the office he barely caught a glimpse of Holly, landing on the bottom stair, sickle in one hand and Artemis's covered cage in the other, when the world seemed to explode around them. He heard several things at once: Melody's scream as hot magic scorched her like fire from a flame thrower, Holly yelling a warning at him, and her familiar's screeching terror. All at once the room spun and blasts of blue flame engulfed them.

"Holly," he yelled but his throat tightened and no noise came out of him. The blue light intensified to white and from the glaring center stepped a single, black robed figure.

Master Renault. "Kneel before me, subject, so that I may claim your life."

Max fell to his knees, the crushing weight of the other's magic pushing him down. He tried to fight it, but it was little use.

"No!" Holly burst through the miasma and pushed forward to stand beside him. He immediately felt the other Reaper's magic falter slightly and the magic upon him lessened.

"Leave, little one, lest I pour my wrath upon you," Georges ground out, clearly struggling with maintaining the powerful magic he wielded.

"Let him go," she called out, her own strength wavering at her effort. "You will not claim this one. The Council has not ruled."

"I no longer care for what your weak council has declared or not. They cast me out, throw me to the winds as though I have no value at all. I have no need for your pitiful guild. I have power on my own. And when I deliver your Immortal to those that have called for his soul, no guild, Reaper or otherwise will have sanction over me."

The old Reaper's fury flared and his energy renewed. The white light increased and Max's skin burned as the magic started to deconstruct his very soul. Just as he felt he was about to fly apart, something changed.

Renault's power suddenly waned and Max fell forward as if he were a marionette whose strings had been cut. Landing on his face, he felt the foyer's soft carpet, the cool breeze from the open door, and the early evening dimness replaced the boiling white light.

"Max?"

Suddenly, Holly was beside him, pulling him over so that his head rested in her lap. Caressing his face, he saw the mixture of fear and relief touching her expression.

"I'm fine," he croaked, though he was pretty sure he wasn't. "What just happened?"

"He tried to force-Reap you. Thankfully, he's not strong enough yet to complete the task."

Surprise and anxiety burst within him and he sat up. "You mean he's going to get stronger? How is this possible?"

She shrugged. "I don't know all the details, but he's gone rogue."

"Reapers can do that? I mean, he's gone beyond crazy, here. He's gone bat crap crazy."

She sat back. "I know, and he's got help somehow. Someone on the Council is betraying the other two, I think. That's the only way this could even have occurred. But, that's not the worst of it."

"There's more?"

She nodded. "He's found some other magic. Not of our guild or any other I know of. He means to rule all the guilds, I think. And if he does, then there will be war."

Holly's thoughts spun at everything she'd just learned. Her longtime friend and mentor was a madman with a bent toward megalomania. He posed a great danger not only to her entire guild, but also the innocent people he'd destroy in the wake of his insane campaign. And the man she now held in her arms, Max. Whatever sins he'd committed in his past, he had no part in any of this.

But it was more than that. It was the stealing of power that threatened the very landscape of magic.

"Hey," Max said as he struggled to his feet. "Your idea about getting out of here still a viable option?"

Holly nodded. "It won't put him off forever, but if we can get out of his way for a bit, we might be able to figure something out."

Just then another staggered into the room.

"Melody?" Max paled at the sight of her.

The vibrant young witch was visibly diminished. Her petite frame appeared slenderer, her complexion wan. Her hair had lost its luster and her gown was torn and scorched in places, but the fire in her expression didn't dim in the slightest.

"I did what I could," she said. "I cast a spell of separation. It'll keep him away from her for a time but he's very resistant. You need to get to safety."

Holly climbed to her feet and nodded. "When he comes

back, he'll be a lot stronger and even more determined than before. The question is, where can we go?"

Max cleared his throat, and her attention went immediately to him. "What is it?"

"I know a place but you won't like it."

"If it will get us out of Renault's way for a while, I'm game."

He gave her a dry laugh. "You say that now. Just wait."

Max walked toward her and she saw he was limping. Although he was doing a fine job trying to hide it, she'd been trained to assess her subject's overall health.

"You're hurt," she said, stepping toward him and pulling his arm over her shoulder, helping him to the door.

"It's nothing. It's just a strained muscle in my leg."

Fear shot through Holly's chest. Was it possible?

"Let me look at it," she said. Grabbing his pant leg, she pulled the scorched fabric apart. That was when she saw it.

"Well?" Max asked.

The witch leaned forward. "Is that what I think is?" she whispered.

Holly's mouth went dry. It was going to be very hard to tell him but she was sure he'd know immediately if she lied.

"It's bad," she said at last. "You've been marked," she told him. She pointed out the Celtic circle now burned into his flesh.

"I don't understand."

"It's a remnant from the old days," she told him. "Back when the old Reapers would have to chase down their subjects. A life could be bought and sold. If a Reaper wanted to hold a subject in thrall, he would mark the poor soul and then force the thrall to do his will. Sometimes they would act as protectors for the Reapers, even sacrificing themselves under threat of the Reaper attacking their family."

"Seriously?"

She shook her head. "Thankfully, times have changed. The worst you'll get is an ugly scar."

To her surprise, Max gave her a dry laugh. "I always wanted a tattoo," he joked.

"This is serious."

He leaned forward wearing a lopsided grin. "What? I'm half serious. I was thinking a cool snake, or maybe an awesome dragon..."

"Beg pardon," Melody said beside them. "You need to go now. He's coming back. I'll hold him off as long as I can."

"Right." She turned to Max. "Can we get to this place by car? Or, do you have another form of transportation? Because, you know, slipping to an ethereal plane would be really cool right now."

"Sorry, Reaper girl. I told you, the only magic I have is not dying. We can use your rental or my Ferrari."

"Wait, you have a sports car? And we were riding around in converted hearse?"

He shrugged. "It's not just any sports car. It's a statement of my identity and I had a thing for Magnum P.I., back in the eighties."

"Your car is good. Just in case we need to drive fast. But, you're not going to be able to drive with that wound."

"I was afraid you'd say that. Sacrifices must be made."

The moment he started to move forward, he faltered and it took both her and the witch to get him out to the garage and into the small Italian car.

"Yeesh," she huffed. "You barely fit in here."

"Good thing I'm all bendy." He gave her a lopsided grin.

It was a good thing they got him in the car when they did, because even with both women helping, he was becoming more and more unwieldy by the minute.

"He's getting worse," Holly said.

"Is that normal?"

"No. It's the after effect of Renault's attack."

An expression of concern covered the witch's face. "Will it kill him?"

"Only if the old Reaper wants him dead, but I don't think that's the case. The old goat needs him alive. I think the magic he's seeking will come at the moment of Max's death."

"I don't understand," Melody said. "What power could he possibly gain at the death of another?"

That was when Holly realized just what her former mentor was up to. She swallowed. "By stealing Max's magic at the time of death, it will increase Renault's power exponentially. It's one of the reasons the Council is so strict with Immortals."

"I thought Reapers were immortal," Melody said as Holly slid into the sleek driver's seat.

"We are long lived, a reward for dealing in death, I suppose. But immortality for a Reaper is far different than most other races, human or Magic. Immortality increases a Reaper's power a thousand-fold. Renault is trying to change the very fabric of life and death."

"To what end?"

"Who knows what a madman can do if he has enough power?"

"Right," Melody said. "I'll notify the authorities. We might not be powerful enough to take him out, but at least we can maybe hold him off for a little while."

With that, Holly threw the car into gear and pulled out of the drive.

"Where are we going, big guy?" she called to Max.

His color was fast draining from his face and a fine sheen of sweat broke out on his brow. Obviously in a great deal of pain, he ground his jaw. "Underworld City," he breathed. "It's on the GPS." He struggled to lift his hand and point to the dashboard unit. "I don't know how long I can fight it off," he said at last.

"He's only wounded you. Once we get a few miles out of town, I'll cast a spell of ease so you can have a little respite from the pain."

Despite her assurances, she wasn't sure he even heard them. Glancing to her left, she saw that he'd already slipped from consciousness.

CHAPTER FIFTEEN

MAX KNEW HE WAS IN huge trouble. More than he'd ever been in his life before, in fact. He also knew he should be more concerned than he was.

Except that there he was, with a beautiful woman beside him, fretting about him and doing her best to keep him alive. Heaven help him, that made her so awesome that he could hardly believe it. The simple fact was, she liked him. A lot.

Of course, he'd had girlfriends in the past. In almost every time period, he'd had the interest of one lady or another. Nowhere near the hot dog womanizer his brother was, Max didn't have to go long without female companions if he didn't want to.

But Holly was different. Something in her drew him like no woman he'd ever known. Driven, brilliant, and strong-willed, he'd realized that he'd been taken by her from the very first moment they'd met. More than that, he knew that he'd little care for his immortality, except that staying alive meant only one thing.

More time to spend with Holly.

"Hey," he heard her say beside him. Her voice garbled and echoed strangely in his ears. "I know you're having a hard time, probably feeling pretty weird, but that's the toxin that Renault gave you."

"I thought maybe I'd already died." A coughing fit came over him then, and it was several gasping moments before he managed to bring his breathing back to normal.

"Easy. We should be there soon. Um, wherever it is you've sent us, that is."

He let out another breath. "It's my brother's place. I didn't have time to warn him, though. Tough to know what kind of welcome we'll get."

"You'd think he'd be accommodating. After all, if you die, so does he, right?"

"That's how it works," he said. "I'm sorry for putting you through all this."

She gasped. "You're sorry? I'm the one who tried to Reap you. If I hadn't called Renault in the first place..."

"You were doing your job. You said it yourself, some people don't have the decency to die when they should. I'm just overdue."

"Nonsense. You are not to blame for this. I'm not sure anybody is. Madness just happens. And when it combines with evil, well, that's when bad things happen."

In that moment, Max didn't think he could ever love anyone more.

And he knew he had to tell her what he felt before time ran out and he lost his ability to do so.

"Listen," he said. "I don't know how this is going to end, but if I do die, I don't want you feeling responsible for me. I've lived for centuries and I'm okay if it ends now. Of course, I'd be really disappointed in not getting to spend more time with you."

There, he'd said it.

"I feel the same way," she said, and he was pretty sure that he heard regret in her tone despite the distortion. "Stop it. I'm not ready to let you go, so we're going to fix this. I promise."

"I love that you think that."

"I don't just 'think' it, I mean to make it happen. No matter what."

The tone of determination he heard from her struck a chord deep within him.

Closing his eyes, he remembered others who had sacrificed themselves for people and causes they believed in.

"Wait," he said, struggling to sit up straighter in the car seat. "Don't you dare do it."

"Do what?" Despite her feigned ignorance, he knew she understood his concern.

"Don't sacrifice yourself for me. I'm not worth it."

She laughed, but it wasn't real humor, even with his wavering hold on hearing, he could tell the difference.

"Don't worry. I've no plans to give in to Renault, to save you or anyone else."

He shook his head and it felt like tin marbles had been set rolling in his brain. "I mean it. I'm ready to die, but not because I'm ready to lose you. My life or death will have no meaning if you go first."

"I..." she started, but didn't finish.

"Promise me you won't try to trade your life for mine."

She let out a breath. "Reapers have a code, you know. We have to protect our charges until we help them cross into the beyond."

"Well, here's a news flash for you. If you're trying to keep me alive, then you've already forsaken your Reaper-ness."

Was that right? It felt correct, but darkness was encroaching on his mind and he doubted he would have the strength to argue much more.

"Max, please."

"No. I mean it. Do me this one solid. Don't die because of me." He coughed again. "In fact, don't die, period."

He heard her sniffle and though his vision was failing, he saw her drag her arm across her face. "Fine. No dying for me. But you better fight hard to stay alive, or I won't forgive you."

"Cross your heart and hope to live?"

Well, he'd thought it was funny. If he was going to go out, he wanted to at least be spouting sarcasm.

"I do. Silly Immortal," she said. "Try to rest."

As the car turned a final corner, Max felt the usual heavy atmosphere of darkness form around them.

"Tell my brother I said hi..."

That was the very last of his strength and he felt his thoughts evaporate like steam in a rainforest. One by one, his senses left him. First, his sight narrowed to a small point of light, winking out like a burned-out Christmas tree light. Then, the warbling sounds of the car engine, Holly's breath and his own heart beats, diminished until there was no more sound. Max became numb, and the warm scent of the Italian upholstery no longer soothed his sense of smell.

He was alone, separate from everything, and it was pure torture. That was the gift the old Reaper had given him. Existence without form, a living death of sorts, and one in which he knew he could not escape.

But Holly would stay by his side no matter what. He'd heard her say so before the last of his hearing had left him. No matter what Renault had planned, something good came out of his evil intentions. Max and Holly found each other.

Whether for eternity or for a few years, any time with Holly was more than worth it. Max would have traded a dozen lives to be with her.

She's worth it all, was his last thought as his consciousness popped out of existence.

The car roared into the driveway, and all Holly could think about was Max. He'd passed out minutes earlier and panic grew within her every moment since. Even though she wasn't sure he could even hear her, she talked to him, telling him about her life before becoming a Reaper. About the death of her parents, her sister getting into trouble and the foster parents who'd rescued both of them and given her the opportunity to make something better of herself.

But now more than ever, she knew that had been her worst mistake. She'd chosen the wrong profession and had no one to blame for it but herself. And now, realizing it had suddenly set something right inside her.

Deep down, she realized she'd known it all along. And she suspected Renault had known it as well. Was it possible he'd been planning this for decades? That he'd manipulated her to keep her in the job so that he could later make her part of his plans in his quest for power?

"How could I be so stupid?" she asked the silent car.

Her thoughts were interrupted by someone beating on the car window. Looking up, she saw Matty standing there, his face bearing the same moist sheen that had covered Max, and even under the dim streetlight, she saw that he had paled as well.

Rolling down the window, she looked into the eyes that were so like and yet unlike Max's. "We need to get this car out of sight."

He nodded and pointed her to a copse of trees just past the driveway.

"My neighbor won't mind us using his shop."

Nodding, Holly put the car back in gear and slowly drove around behind the trees to see a small garage off to the side of the property.

Ten minutes later, she had it parked was opening the car door, doing her best to keep a limp, unconscious Max from plummeting to the ground.

"I need help," was all she managed before both of them fell backwards. Max rolled out and was now slumped into her lap, his arms and legs akimbo.

"Right."

Just then, Holly heard the roar of a motorcycle engine growing in the distance. She and Matty were struggling to get Max off of Holly, when the bike pulled into the drive way. The figure that stepped forward was that of a tall, slender woman. Dressed in a black leather jacket and pants, wearing knee-high boots and a black helmet, the woman climbed off the machine and walked over to them.

Werewolf.

Holly had not Reaped any magical beings being assigned to humans primarily, but like any magical being, she knew others when they approached. Were-beings, Witches, Warlocks, Fae and the like were as clear to her senses as the flowers or trees.

Having been raised alongside and later working amongst the Magics, the one race that put a hitch in her chest was the werewolf.

"Matty? What is it? What's wrong?"

"Hey, baby. I'm so glad you came. Things are bad. Very bad."

"Max?" she asked as she knelt on Max's opposite side. "What's wrong with him?" She looked up at the twin. "With them?"

Before Holly could speak, Matty cleared his throat. "She's Max's new squeeze. Came here to Reap him, um, us."

"That true?"

Holly let out a breath. "In the beginning, yes. But not now. My former mentor has gone insane. He's trying to pull in the power of the Immortals to add to his own. We're not sure what he means to do with it. Kinda crazy."

"I see."

"Can you help us get him inside? He's very heavy."

Just then, thunder sounded and in the distance the landscape lit up with lightning."

"Is that the guy?" Matty asked. "Is he coming for us now?"

"Calm down," the Werewolf snapped. "It's a storm coming. Saw it on the weather channel."

"Right. We should get him indoors." Matty started to stoop down but the woman put out her hand.

"I've got this."

Then, like she was lifting an infant from the ground, she slid her hands under Max picked him up.

"Wow," Holly muttered, suddenly free of his weight.

"Let's go," she said, turning toward the house without waiting for them.

Matty started to falter just as Max had earlier. Scrambling to her feet, she took hold of him and threw his arm over her shoulder to help him stay upright. Following in the werewolf's footsteps, they made it into the house, through a small kitchen and into the main living room.

"Over there," the werewolf said pointing to a chaise as she gently laid Max on the sofa.

Doing as she was told, she helped the twin to settle.

"Thanks, babe. I knew you'd come."

"Ha," the woman scoffed. "If I hadn't gotten the call from the witch I wouldn't have known. And, for the record, I'm doing this for your brother, not for your worthless hide."

"She really is crazy about me," Matty grinned. "Just doesn't want to admit it."

"Right."

Holly turned to the Werewolf. "I'm Holly Dent." She held out her hand and waited while the other woman pulled off her helmet and jacket. Hair as black as midnight and jade colored eyes, she was the classic werewolf beauty.

"Fiona O'Malley." She took Holly's hand and gave it a too tight but thankfully brief handshake. "So, you're the Reaper girl that's finally turned ol' Max's head, huh?"

Holly felt her face heat up and suddenly she was back in high school, mooning over her latest crush. Still, she straightened her spine and faced the other woman.

"Good. He needs somebody. And if you're here protecting him, that means you're probably the one."

"I hope we have long enough to find out."

Fiona nodded. "You're safe enough for the time being. Though, if this guy is strong enough to threaten these guys, then you might want to be coming up with a plan."

That was the rub, Holly thought. "I'm not strong enough to take him face on." She glanced over to Max. "And, I made a promise," she began.

"Whatever you do," Matty said, struggling to stay upright. "Can you fix this spell the old rat put on us?"

"That is something I can do." She went to Max's side and knelt. Placing her hand on his cool, damp brow, she couldn't help but feel a surge of emotion — fear, anger, hope and love. But none of that would help her with the task ahead.

"Can you make some tea and something to eat? This is a very draining procedure and once the men are settled, they'll need some food and drink as well."

"On it," Fiona said, pulling out her cell phone. "I personally don't cook, but I can have food delivered — I own the local tavern. Sustenance will be arriving shortly."

Once she'd turned away, Holly went to work.

The transfer of power was a simple thing, and one of the few Reaper duties that she excelled at. As a rule, people thought when you died, you just diminished, or faded into nothingness. But, many times people in poor condition rallied at the last moment. When a doctor or nurse said someone needed to 'get better to die,' it wasn't always in jest.

And when they needed help Holly was there. What Max and his brother needed more than anything was her strength. Thankfully, that was one thing that she had in abundance.

Taking Max's hands in both of hers, she began to chant, the words drawing forth her inner power, hoping beyond hope it would be enough to make him better.

His words returned to her. *"You're an empath. You take on the pain of others and make it your own."*

"Give me your pain," she whispered to him and then opened herself to him.

"The blasted bowels of Beelzebub!" Renault shouted across the small hotel room. "Who the devil do they think they are, daring to cross a Reaper of the first level?"

Cravens pushed into the room, arms laden with ointments, oils and new bandages. "She scorched your best robe, my lord. I'm doing what I can to repair it..."

The old Reaper waved his hand. "As if I care for such things. Get me one of the older ones. I need to eat and renew my strength. Witches are such dirty fighters. Came at me when I wasn't expecting it. Wait until I finish with the Immortals. Then no one will be able to cross me again."

His servant bobbed his head and the sight of him only added to Renault's fury. He was sore and was burning at his humiliation. The urge to strike out at Craven was almost overwhelming, but for now he needed his minion.

Thirty minutes later, after eating and drinking some strong tea, the old Reaper regained some of his strength. "It won't be long now," he told his servant. "And I will dispense with them all."

CHAPTER SIXTEEN

HAVING LIVED A VERY LONG time, and having never in all that time ever been unable to lose himself so completely, when Max felt Holly's strength ebbing into him, it was a completely new experience. One moment he was lost in velvet darkness, his thoughts extinguished like the wick of a candle. His soul without existence.

He'd been floating in a tunnel of nothingness and she'd extended a line to him. He felt much like an astronaut floating in zero-G. She was his tether and thankfully, the stronger her power got, the closer she could pull him.

And, suddenly, there she was. Talking to him with words he didn't understand. But the sound of her voice caressed his senses, awakening them one by one until he was almost fully returned to himself.

"There you are, sleepyhead," Holly muttered over him. "Welcome back to the world of the living."

He sent her a weak smile. "How long was I out?"

"Awhile," she said. "But not to worry, you're back now."

He looked around the room and saw his brother on the chaise. "Oh. How long has he been out?"

"Not as long as you, but close. He started showing symptoms not long after we got here. Renault has to be stopped."

"You have no argument from me."

"But we can't do it here. In our realm, he has more power than we do."

Max shook his head to clear it. "But you're a Reaper. If what you say is true, that means we have no hope."

He watched her let out a breath, her spirit seeming to diminish as she did so. "Physical power? He is older and of a different class than me. Our powers are more uneven because of the type of subjects we Reap. He was a Reaper of the first class, which means he dealt with the most powerful of Magics. Whereas I have more flexibility than he does because I generally Reap those of lesser power, but which are far more mainstream."

Max watched her expression. "What about in determination? Are you more stubborn than he is?"

That comment took her by surprise. "What do you mean?"

"I know you can't tell it now, with me in this weakened condition, but I'm a pretty braw fighter myself. Hand to hand, fist to fist, sword to sword, none of that mattered to me. I would take any challengers, even those that were bigger and meaner. I won every time."

"Of course you'd survive. You're an Immortal."

He laughed. "But that didn't mean I didn't feel the impact of every fist, the cut of every blade. Sure, I lived, but it wasn't always a picnic. I took my share of beatings resulting in broken bones, bruised muscles, and damaged organs. None of which are very pleasant to endure."

He hadn't meant his tone to become morose, but he wanted her to know that though it seemed he'd lead a charmed existence, it wasn't all it was cracked up to be.

"You've suffered," she said at last. "I've known so many who'd begged for death to come. I'm sorry."

Her sincerity went right through to his heart. She truly

did understand his plight. Thankfully, he wasn't the sort to dwell on his own life's misfortune.

Shrugging, he waved her off. "My point was that there was one thing that helped me win contests against those bigger, stronger and better fighters than I." He leaned forward and waggled his eyebrows in an attempt to lighten the mood.

"What's that?"

"I refuse to give up."

She blinked at that. "Is that all?" She laughed, then covered her mouth, obviously surprised by her own reaction.

He nodded. "I know it seems simplistic and I'd be laughing too, if I didn't know it to be the truth."

She eyed him for a moment. "I don't doubt you. It's just, Renault is not your usual opponent. And his magic is so much stronger than mine. I doubt I could best him."

"I don't doubt you." He leaned forward, gently caressing her chin. "From the moment you showed up on my doorstep, I suspected you were a most determined lady. You won't go down without a fight. And, fighting is something I know about."

She hesitated, looking down at her hands for a moment. He could feel the struggle boiling inside her. Clouds gathered outside and the room darkened.

The pall didn't last, and gradually the clouds outside cleared and sunlight returned.

"I'm not sure I believe you, but I believe *in* you. I promise I won't give up, no matter what the cost."

He hadn't realized it before that very moment how much he adored her. Fascinated by her magnificent emerald gaze, drawn even closer by her scent of wildflowers and warm moist breath upon his cheek.

"I want to kiss you, again," he said, surprised by the urgency of his desire.

He felt her sigh deep in his soul.

She surprised him by pulling back. "I want you to, believe me. But..."

His heart froze in his chest. Did she not want the same? "What?"

"It's not a good time. We're going to need all of our strength if we're going to beat him."

Relief flooded through him. She wasn't rejecting him outright. Max chuckled.

"You're right, but it's going to be tough to wait. On the other hand, getting the chance to kiss you is going to shore up my determination that once this is over, you and I have some serious catching up to do in the romance department."

"Oh," she said, her face turning a most pleasant pink. So sweet was her embarrassment, that Max vowed right then and there to stay alive if only to see the pleasing color as often as possible.

"Now, as to the defeating Renault part," he said, clearing his throat. "There is one thing I insist you agree to."

"Which is?"

"You have to stay alive. I'll not have you sacrificing yourself for me."

She shook her head, her color now deepening even further as her anger became evident. "You've no right to tell me what to do." Then, suddenly realizing what he was saying, she pulled back. "Of course, I have no intention of doing anything so foolish. But, if you go down, we go down together. And, it's my choice, not yours."

He pulled her close once again. "Don't misunderstand me. I'm not planning on running into the abyss all willy nilly. I'm going to fight to stay alive right beside you. But, if it looks like you can't win, like we can't win, then fate must be allowed its reign. You're young with what I hope to be an eternity ahead of you. I've lived a very long time."

"Max, please," she began.

He held up his right hand. "On this, I'm solid. You are not allowed to die."

Holly was about to speak, but before she could, a loud moan sounded from the other Immortal in the room.

"Seriously? Do you have to keep going on like that?" he groaned. "Just get busy saving us, Reaper girl."

"Matty," Max growled.

"No," Holly said. "He's right. We really don't have time to argue."

The front door swung open and their hostess stepped through. "I just got a call from one of my guys on the watcher's post. There is a whole bunch of magic energy headed this way. I think your crazy Reaper enemies are headed out this way."

Icy fear stabbed into Max's heart — a pain not for himself, but rather for Holly. She pushed away from him and stood up.

"It's time to face our enemies. Let's get going. I need my scythe and my familiar." With that, Holly straightened her clothes and stepped past Fiona, walking to the door.

Stunned for only a moment, Max jumped to his feet. "Let's go guys. Time is of the essence."

Matty scratched his head. "Now, that's something you don't hear from an Immortal every day." He paused. "Or, ever."

"I think she's pretty serious," Fiona said beside him. "You better get going, Maxi. I'm afraid she's going to leave you behind. Matty and I will be right behind you."

"Right."

Max heard his brother hiss behind him. "Wait. Does this mean we're a couple again?"

"Shut up," Fiona said behind him.

Sure enough, he had to quick step to get to the car just as she brought the engine to life. A few seconds later he was seat-belted into the passenger's seat and headed into what was likely going to end in his death.

Despite that, he couldn't help the thrill of fighting at her side. The stakes were high but deep in his marrow he knew that if anyone could save them both, it was Holly.

Live or die, he was grateful for whatever time they had together and he meant to make the most of it. No matter what the cost.

It was well after dark when they pulled into the funeral home's parking lot. The front door that suffered damage during Renault's attack had been boarded up with plywood and the fragmented glass was cleaned up. A pang of regret went through Holly. The stately home had been so beautiful and it hurt to see it so molested.

"Max," she said quietly, gently touching his sleeve.

Though she was sure he didn't want to admit it, the Reaper's attack had taken a far deeper toll than he let on. They'd barely been on the highway ten minutes before he fought to keep from falling asleep. She'd urged him to rest, telling him that he needed as much strength as possible if they were going to survive the confrontation. He'd been hesitant, but the low jazz she played on the car radio, and the tedious miles slipping by had done the trick. Before they were a mile out of town, he slipped into quiet slumber until she roused him again.

"Hmm?" His eyes fluttered open and in the next moment, panic covered his expression as he shook out of sleep-induced confusion.

"It's okay. We're back." She pointed to the funeral home.

He let out a breath, relaxing back into his seat and rubbing his eyes. "Already," he muttered. "That didn't take long."

"No. And, I don't feel any energy surges nearby, so we should be okay to run inside and grab my stuff."

"Right." He moved to open the door but she held out her hand.

"I'll get them. You wait here and rest up."

He touched her arm and she felt his breath come out in a rush. "Don't be too long," he said.

"I won't," she said.

Heart pounding, she slid out of the car and made her way up the front steps. Nearly midnight, the sky above was clear, but her fear stirred the atmosphere, and by the time she reached the front door, the sky filled with clouds, making the darkness feel all the more oppressive around her. Fortunately, she didn't need much light, since her own internal senses were acute. A few minutes more, and she had the tools that helped concentrate her magic — her scythe and her familiar.

"It's about time," Artemis's voice filtered into Holly's thoughts. "You've no idea what's been going on around here. Your friend has sent his underling here twice looking for you and your boyfriend."

Holly let out a breath. "I'm sure. Which is why we don't have much time."

"You're going to do it, aren't you? You're going to try and save him."

"Yes."

Holly reached the top stair and threw open her bedroom door. Bright light stung her eyes, but she pushed forward toward the room's only occupant.

The bird ruffled its feathers, sending dust and dander out in a cloud of luminescent white. "I was afraid you were going to say that. No way I can talk you out of it?"

"I love him," Holly said, voicing the words that had

been growing in her heart since the moment they'd met.

She felt the energy increase around her. "Foolish humans," the bird huffed. "There was no way to do this without drawing attention to us. You're going to need my help, you know."

"I'm counting on it."

Suddenly the light faded and where the bird had once been perched upon its stand, there now sat a petite figure, a light sprite. Her head was covered in fine, soft feathers, but her face, arms and legs were flesh. She had small, white feathers as eyebrows, but her eyes and mouth were a perfect pink and when she smiled, it was clear that what had once been her beak had now receded inward and become teeth.

"Oh," Holly breathed. She'd always known her friend had the ability to shift to semi-human form. Still, watching her do so was truly breathtaking.

"Ready to do this?" Artemis asked.

Artemis, Holly thought, suddenly remembering Greek mythology, the goddess of war. She never realized it, but her friend was one of the most decorated warriors of all time.

Holly knew a familiar could increase her powers when the circumstances warranted it. She'd never known how or why and had never thought to ask. The Reaper was always simply grateful.

"Your highness," Holly bowed before her.

The shifter ruffled its remaining feathers. "No need to suck up. The time of Gods and Goddesses has passed. I'm simply a shifter with precious few powers these days. Besides, it's I who should be bowing to you, Reaper. You've given me purpose these many years past and I've mostly enjoyed your company."

"What can you do to help me?" Holly would have liked

to learn more about her mysterious friend, but there simply wasn't time for it. "Can you help me fight Renault?"

"Oh heavens, no. Not in the traditional sense. I'm afraid that battle is between the two of you. As it is, I can barely hold on to this plane. What I can do, is combine my senses with yours, so to speak. I'm able to hear the thoughts of others and that may be helpful. Any foreshadowing of what that old goat is up to may be helpful."

"Right." Of course, Artemis would be the better fighter in her own right. She'd been among the strongest of her ilk. There'd been stories that she'd out maneuvered her enemies at every turn so that when she drew her sword, her cut was deadly.

"Good. The Immortal grows restless. It's time..."

Suddenly, the room shook around them and Holly fell to the floor. A loud crashing sound cut through the room.

Artemis gasped. "He's here. That devil has arrived." She covered her ears and crouched low to protect herself.

Holly didn't wait to ask what happened because deep inside, she knew. "Max!" she screamed, and scrambling to her feet, she grabbed her scythe and headed for the door. Without looking, she knew Artemis had taken flight again and was close behind.

Taking the steps two at a time she bounded down, but with the house shaking around her, it was impossible to keep her footing. By the time she was half way down, she was bouncing from side to side, the sharp edges of the stairs striking her as she tucked and rolled to the bottom.

The atmosphere roared a result of a battle between the Magical realm and the earthly one. Just as Holly made the bottom stair, a piece of the wood mantle broke loose and, even though she ducked, it struck her square on her right temple. Dazed, she refused to give in to the encroaching darkness, but instead struggled to stagger to the door.

"Hurry," Artemis whispered into her thoughts. "He's got the Immortal."

Finally, Holly grasped the knob and, using the very last of her strength, she yanked it open. An impossibly bright light shone down from the heavens and in its center was a sight that froze the blood in her veins.

Renault stood, wearing his Reaper gold robes and grasping his silver scythe. A large, oily smile broke through his mad expression.

But that wasn't the worst of it. Beside him was Cravens, the hideous man now enhanced by his master's new powers. Bigger, stronger, and more twisted than Holly remembered. He held in his hands a thick iron chain and when he jerked it forward, another entered the column of light.

"No," Holly barely breathed.

"Leave me," Max said. Beaten, he now was covered in bruises, his right eye blackened, and his mouth cut and swollen. He stood hunched over, his left arm cradling his right, and there was a vicious cut on his right thigh that oozed blood.

"Let him go. He's not yours to Reap."

The other Reaper laughed. "Before I'm finished with him, he'll be begging to leave this mortal coil. When he does, then I know you won't let him suffer."

"You can't do this."

"I can and I will. The High Council is in shreds and they're powerless to do anything about it. Now, do the merciful thing and let me have him."

Holly bit her lip and using her scythe to lean on, stepped forward. "I will not. I challenge you, former Master Renault. As a present member of the Reaper Guild, I command you to turn loose that subject. You will stand down."

The light grew brighter and even from ten feet away, she felt the scorching heat. From the circle, Max cried out.

"Do you really want this? You could be my second, you know. Help me change the fabric of magic for all."

"Please," she said again, her resolve crumbling like sand being wiped away by the surf. "You can't do this. I beg you, let him go."

"Holly, please," Max strangled out. "There's a way to beat him. You know what you must do. Reap me yourself..."

She heard no more. A loud blare sounded and the next thing she knew, the light flashed and then night returned. Renault, Cravens, and Max were gone, and no evidence of them ever being there remained.

"No," she screamed, falling forward.

The blackness covered her like a lead-lined quilt. Max was right and it broke her heart. Now that Renault had him, he could do as he liked. Anything but kill him that was. As her subject, only Holly could do that. And, that was the last thing she would ever do.

It never occurred to Renault that it would be so easy claiming the Immortal. He'd felt the man's presence the moment they'd pulled into the funeral home's drive.

"There he is," Cravens said, the ever-vigilant servant. "Shall we move in, sir?"

"Yes." The car eased up the road, lights dim, the only noise that of the quiet hum of the engine. "But, stay quiet. I don't want to lose him again."

"Yes, sir."

When they finally came within viewing distance, it was immediately clear that his attention was turned toward the house. Fortunately, the Reaper was not with him — close, but far enough, perfect for what the old Reaper had planned.

"Let's go."

The two quietly slipped out of the rental car and approached the Ferrari. Stealth was on their side. When they arrived at the back of the car, Renault went to the driver's side and he motioned his employee to go to the other. He didn't want the Immortal to escape.

Once they were in place, Renault gently tapped the window. The man inside dozed, no doubt a result of the spell the Reaper had cast earlier. While he couldn't outright kill the Immortal, he could slow him down considerably.

The Immortal stirred from his sleep. Bleary-eyed he quickly turned around and saw Renault standing beside the car. He started to jerk away, but it was too late because Cravens had already unlocked the passenger side door and grabbed the Immortal. A few minutes of wrestling and the henchman prevailed, pinning the Immortal to the ground.

"You can't do this," he said. "The only person who can Reap me is Holly, and she's not going to do it."

Renault smiled. "Oh, you'd be surprised at what she might do with the proper incentive."

The other man remained still for a moment, narrowing his eyes. "What is it you want? Why do this?"

The old Reaper thought for a moment. He had his reasons, sure enough. All the times he'd been taken for granted. The long hours he'd worked, the centuries without the slightest recognition.

"I want what's mine. What should have been mine from the beginning."

The other man looked at him, narrowing his eyes and scrutinizing Renault in a way that made him feel like his skin was being pulled off, layer after layer of muscle and bone bared until his soul lie open and bleeding.

"You underestimate her. Holly is far stronger than you or the Council have ever guessed. True, she hides it well, but if you bothered to look close enough, you'd see it."

"Nonsense." Renault turned away, but said nothing else.

Was it possible? Was there more to his former student than he'd ever suspected?

No, he thought. She was weak. She carried the weight of empathy for all her clients and that very thing alone kept her from true strength. No one could be a leader without strength.

He heard the Immortal sigh behind him.

"Fine. Don't believe me. But, you're making a huge mistake."

Turning back, Renault gave him a sharp look. "We'll see who's making the mistake here, Immortal. It's a waste of time discussing this with you. In a few hours, you will no longer be a problem. Perhaps you can learn respect in the next realm, eh?"

Despite his threats, the Immortal appeared unshaken, which told the old Reaper that he was likely stupid or a fool. It didn't matter. Once he was gone and Master Georges absorbed his power, no one could stop him and at last, the ruling council of Reapers would be no more.

CHAPTER SEVENTEEN

"REAPER DENT," MELODY CALLED FROM the door. "There's a lady and an, um gentleman here to see you."

Holly looked up from her reference book in Max's library. She needed information before attempting to rescue him. Time was short and an interruption was the last thing she needed right now. Of course, there might be a chance it was someone with useful information, so she didn't want to dismiss them without even asking.

"Show them in," she said at last.

The door opened and Max's brother and his girlfriend walked through.

"We came as soon as we heard he'd been taken," Fiona said. "What's going to happen now?"

Matty cleared his throat. "I'm not sure. He hasn't been Reaped because I'm still here."

Holly sighed and closed the book in front of her. It hadn't been any help anyway.

"Renault can't Reap Max unless I give him permission. So, for now he's safe. Well, relatively safe, anyway."

"What does that mean?" Matty asked.

Fiona held up her hand. "He might not be comfortable but he's alive."

She sent a knowing glance toward Holly.

"I just need to find him."

"You don't know where he's taken him?" Matty moved forward, his face turning even more pale. At first she'd thought it was fear, but then another thought occurred to her. While the Master Reaper couldn't kill Max, he could drain his magic. Bit by bit, but the longer he was in the madman's care, the more dangerous it became for him. While it was true, you couldn't kill an Immortal, you could make them so weak that they no longer wished to go on.

And that would be the worst tragedy of all.

But there was a good side to it. Clearly, the two of them were linked and Holly could discern his brother's condition by watching Matty.

"What do we do now?" Fiona asked, stepping forward, taking Matty's arm and giving him her support without making it too obvious.

"We have to find him. When we spoke last, he was at the Hotel Chalet. A small inn on the outskirts of town."

"Really?" Fiona asked. "That place has been booked up for months. In fact, they start booking a week after the festival."

"Which means he's been planning this for a long time," Holly said. Again, a wave of guilt washed over her. She was the reason he'd come to Nocturne Falls. He'd probably had something to do with her being assigned to Max in the first place.

He'd been manipulating her from the start.

Fiona pulled out her cell phone and punched a number on its surface. "Hello? Yeah, I need to talk to one of your customers. A Renault. Is he available?"

Holly held her breath as she waited for Fiona's answer. "Come on," she muttered under her breath.

Fiona pulled her phone from her ear and clicked it off.

"There has never been anyone by that name at the hotel. He's in the wind."

Holly's heart sank. She had to find him without letting him know he had her at a disadvantage. In other words, he'd set the stage. The only way she'd be able to locate Max was by giving in.

She would never do that.

"What are we going to do now?" Matty demanded. A fine sheen of sweat covered his brow. His condition was worsening by the minute.

"Matty," Fiona said softly. "Why don't you sit down? You don't look so good."

She sent Holly a worried expression, her fear clearly mirroring Holly's.

"He can't be too far," she said, shaking her head trying to clear it. Then, a thought occurred to her. "So, all the rental properties are filled in town, right?"

Fiona shrugged. "As far as I've heard."

"Right. What about any new residents in Nocturne Falls? This community has been around awhile and I bet you don't get too many people buying up property and setting down roots."

Fiona blinked. "Hardly anybody. Wait, the MacCallister's place on Demonstar Lane," she turned to Matty. "You remember honey? They had the road blocked off when the roofers came last month. Gnarled up traffic for a week."

Matty nodded. His breath grew short and his skin took on a waxy color.

Holly swallowed. "That has to be the place. How long ago was it sold?"

"About a year ago, this month. I remember because the place was in such bad shape. The old warlock who lived there reached the end, you know. Check out time..."

"And I bet an old Reaper showed up to help him cross over."

"I guess. I mean, they didn't come to Underworld, and I have to admit, I don't get out much."

"Fiona..." Matty moaned. Before she could answer, he collapsed and slipped from consciousness.

"Matty!" she cried out. "No. Don't leave me, you jerk. I'll never forgive you if you do..."

Fiona didn't look the type to give into emotions easily, but it was clear she cared for Max's brother.

Holly knew the time for dancing around things had officially passed. She had to face off with the Reaper beast once and for all. She'd likely die in the attempt, but Holly wasn't going to give up without a fight. Besides, she'd rather die than let the cancer that had invaded her guild continue.

"Fiona," she called out softly. The other woman's attention was still on her boyfriend, but she nodded.

"Yes?"

"I need your help. Tell me where this place is. I'm going to find them and end this once and for all."

"Right. I'll come with you." She started to stand but Holly held out her hand.

"There's nothing you can do. Reaper magic can't be affected by other forms of magic. You need to stay here with him and do what you can to give him ease if I fail."

Fiona bit her bottom lip and nodded. "Right." Reaching under her blouse she pulled out a silver amulet. "In case things go south and you need to get out, use this to contact me. Say my name and it will pull you back here."

Holly was touched by the other woman's concern. She started to take the amulet. "Thank you, but if things go south, there will be no coming out for me. If Max crosses over, I go with him."

For the first time since she'd arrived in Nocturne Falls, she gave voice to the depth of her feelings for Max. They'd barely started their relationship and though she'd never expected anything like this to happen, she felt it through to her very soul.

She loved Max and he loved her. They'd fight together. They'd win or lose together. And if she failed, she'd gladly follow him across the veil.

After all, that's what true love was.

"Master Renault?"

The Reaper's servant had been keeping watch at the front gate when he emerged from the mansion.

"Any sign of her yet?"

"No, sir."

Renault paced, doing his best to understand what had just occurred. "It's not possible."

"Sir?" The other man gave him a blank expression. "Are you ill?"

The old Reaper spun around. "Why do you ask that? Do I look sick?"

"You look upset," he began. "But, it could be my imagination." He shrugged. "I'm not a doctor, after all."

"I'm fine," he said after a breath. "She should be here soon."

"How do you know that, sir?"

"Because of her flaw. Her sympathy for others knows no bounds. She will give all to save him a painful death."

"She's already tried to fight you once. Won't she do so again?"

"Even if she does, she can't oppose me for long. I outrank her. She will surrender him if she wants to save our guild."

He didn't know how much time had passed since his abduction, but Max was sure of one thing. His time was running out.

While Renault couldn't kill him outright, he could make him awfully uncomfortable. Like, for instance, the constant painful pull on Max's magic increased by the hour. It was a constant, dull ache and his muscles throbbed, his head about to burst.

He'd tried talking to the wretch, but as it was with the unbalanced, his words had little effect. Renault was taking advantage of Max's weakness so that when Holly finally gave in, as Max knew she eventually would, the transition would be quick — like a scalpel excising a cancer.

He swallowed. Now that wasn't a pleasant thought at all.

"She will give in, you know."

The old man sat upon his throne, an overly large recliner positioned in the center of the room. It was made of expensive leather, as was everything in the oversized room. A gothic mansion, the place had high ceilings and polished marble floors. Whoever had lived there before had quite expensive and exquisite tastes.

"I told you. She's tougher than you think."

"Ah, but her emotions rule her. Holly Dent has a soft center. She'll see you suffering and do the humane thing and send you to the beyond. It's why I chose her, you know. Her sympathetic heart. She'll do what's necessary to end another's pain."

Max knew that was the truth and hoped it didn't get that far. It was a long shot, but he'd already taken measures to keep as healthy as possible for the time being.

Using the nexus that existed between him and his twin, he'd managed to pull some of his brother's magic to add to his own. Although he knew if they ever made it out of this situation, Matty wasn't going to be very happy about it. Hopefully by now he was unconscious and no longer aware of the discomfort.

Max yawned. "This is so boring. You're out to take revenge on those that slighted you, blah, blah, blah..." Maybe baiting the madman wasn't such a good idea, but the more of his anger he directed at Max, the less he would have for Holly.

"You will cease your mockery of me this instant. If not, I'll not make your Reaping so easy."

"I don't think you have the strength, if you did, I'd be rendered unconscious by now."

The Reaper stood to his feet. "Do you dare challenge me, Immortal? You're risking her life as well, you know."

"If you say so, but again, I think she'll surprise you."

With that comment, the Reaper howled in anger. Turning, he reached for his scythe and when he faced Max again, he held it high. Max saw the onslaught of the Reaper's attack a few seconds before he felt it.

The atmosphere charged around him, lights blazed, and a shock of pain lit every nerve in his body. Before he'd met Holly, he would have fast been on his knees begging for the pain to stop. He'd have given his last breath in exchange for sweet release.

But now, knowing what she faced, he would not give in. He would not help this fiend destroy her.

It wasn't just the devastating loss of Max in her life, as bad as that might be. Max knew the sort of power hungry wretch standing before him, and the Reaper would not stop until he vanquished anyone who stood against him — including Holly. Either way, Max was sure the Reaper would surely destroy her, and that, Max would not allow.

Suddenly, the pain eased and disappeared. He was so shaken that he didn't realize at first it was gone, the resonance of his pain still twisting inside him. But when he noticed the lights had again dimmed and the air around him returned to normal, he caught a glimpse of Renault falling back, his face red and his breathing short and labored.

The older man's change lasted only a few moments and soon his color returned to normal and his breathing evened out. Despite his rapid recovery, the Reaper was obviously shaken. He didn't say a word, but backed away slowly. When he reached the door, he spun around and ran from the room.

Only then did Max let out the breath he was holding. There was a way to defeat the old Reaper then, and he was certain he knew how to do it.

Now, if only Holly would agree, they would have a chance to put away the beast once and for all.

CHAPTER EIGHTEEN

IT WAS AN HOUR PAST dark when Holly pulled the rental car into the long drive that led to the Reaper's mansion. A tall, imposing building, it reminded her of one of those broken-down castles from a horror movie. She could easily envision walking down long, dust filled corridors only to be attacked by a terrifying ghost or unrelenting ghoul.

But this wasn't a movie and she wasn't a scared heroine walking into trouble. She was facing the most dangerous Reaper ever born and she had to be ready for his attacks. Despite her avoidance of confrontation in the past, and her mild manner and quiet demeanor, she was not a wallflower. Nothing in her life had brought out the lioness in her the way seeing Max hurt by this villain did. She would see it through. She would thwart Master Georges and bring Max home.

Or she would perish in the attempt.

Taking a final breath, she turned off the car's engine, slipped from the driver's seat and stood beside the car. A gust of wind blew past her. She felt the storm building. The air prickled with electricity and a distant rumbling echoed the emotion stirring within her.

"Come on, Holly," she told herself. "Time to gut up and finish this once and for all."

Turning back to the car, she pulled her scythe from the back seat, and started reciting the mantra that always sent her into full Reaper mode. The clouds stirred in the sky and distant thunder boomed. Multiple shards of lightning crackled all around her. A dim blue light emanated from her talisman and almost instantly, she felt the energy begin to flow, rising like a river during a torrential rain.

It felt both good and bad to be in this state. Excitement swelled at summoning the magic that had helped guide souls. Magic moved through her veins setting her nerves alight. Her senses came alive and every living creature sang to her. She felt life buzzing around her and then located the one soul who was her target...

And that's where the bad came in.

"Max," she whispered. She felt his pain as if it were her own, the constant, raw ache he felt, as if every strip of his flesh was being pulled and twisted.

Walking to the mansion's front entrance, she saw Renault's minion there waiting for her just inside the doorway.

"Follow me," he said.

Without saying a word, she walked behind him, down the long, dark corridor through the old house. Musky scents and crannies left untended too long assailed her senses, and their movement stirred up whorls of dust as they passed.

They came to an impressive spiral staircase that seemed to rise out of nothing before going on forever. It had to be at least three floors, she thought. It had an ornate gold railing and thick marble stairs and along its base were pale yellow track lights.

At long last, the servant led her to a central room. Judging from its two-story high domed ceiling, it must have been a ballroom at one time. From the center of the dome hung an elaborate crystal chandelier. The floor was polished white marble with onyx trim. High glass windows surrounded them and off to one side was a raised dais with thick, crimson drapes hanging behind it.

A light came on over the dais and Holly caught sight of Renault, wearing his shimmering gold robes, a glowing white scythe in his hand, his stance poised to strike his victim.

He was ready to begin the Reaping. Beside him, seated in a high back chair, was Max.

The sight of him nearly broke her, and Holly's breath caught in her throat. He was panting, and it was clear that his condition was worsening, his energy draining by the moment.

"Welcome, Reaper Dent," Renault called out. "So glad you could make it."

Holly clenched her jaw, reining in her anger. "Let him go."

"I will not. I've worked too hard and too long to turn away now."

"Holly," Max said, his voice coarse, his tone raw. "It's okay. I've made my peace. I'm begging you, let me go."

Shock and agony shot through her. "I can't," she told him. "I won't..."

"There's no hope for us, Holly. There never has been." He started to say more but was overcome by a coughing fit. Gasping, he shook his head. "Don't you see?"

She shook her head, eyes suddenly burning, hot tears forming like a pot getting ready to boil over. "You're wrong. I can beat him. We can make this right."

Max shook his head. "I know you want to believe that, but we're too different. Too much is at stake for us to be so selfish." He pulled her into his arms, his warm, solid body felt so good against her and she sought his touch like a ship throwing an anchor into a tumultuous sea.

"I won't let you do this."

"Yes, you will." He pulled her closer, wrapping his arms around her. "When he Reaps me, his powers will weaken. That's when you need to go after him. You're far stronger than you think, Holly. And when you defeat him, his magic will fail and then the Council can deal with him once and for all."

She pushed back from him. "If I do that, you'll die."

"It's okay. I've lived a long time, Holly. I've never had the chance to be the hero, you know."

"But, you've been a soldier, for heaven's sake."

"I've played at war, yes. I could fight, yes. I could be injured and feel the pain of each musket ball, each stab of the bayonet, the burning agony from each bullet, but in the end, I would live. An inconvenience, but no real sacrifice."

Holly felt the steam of her arguments cool against her skin. "I don't want to lose you," she said.

"I feel the same," he said, caressing her face, placing his forehead against hers. "But, I need to do this. You've been a heroine for a very long time, Holly. Every soul you guided through the veil, every kindness you've shown them and every hour you've grieved for their loss. Let me do this."

A thick despair covered her then. She'd lost her parents, her friends, her family, and now she was losing him. She didn't know how she could stand it — how she could go on once he was gone from her life forever.

But, deep within her, she knew he spoke the truth. She also knew she couldn't deny him.

Her heart, already cracked and bruised, was on the verge of shattering.

"Okay," she said in a small, weak voice, the last of the fight going out of her.

He pulled her back into his arms, and she fell against him, her energy waning. She wanted to surrender, to die with him, but she knew that was not possible. The living needed her, her guild needed her, and all the realm needed her. She would not disappoint.

Starting to pull back, she was surprised to find his arms entwining around her once again, his hand finding the back of her neck, and leaning down, his mouth finding hers. He kissed her then, deep and long, gentle and hungry at the same time. Holly barely breathed.

That one kiss would be the completion of their time together and she was powerless to stop it.

❧

"Enough," Renault said from is dais. "It's time to begin the Reaping."

Letting go of Holly was the hardest thing he'd ever done. Finally, he'd found the one person who completed him. One who would love him through eternity and give his life purpose. But now that was ending.

He'd never claimed to be an unselfish man. Immortals rarely were. He'd not been unkind, or thoughtless when it came to others, but neither had he been particularly sympathetic.

He'd given plenty of his money to charities over the years, but what did money, or any earthly thing mean to one who lived forever? Fortunes rose and fortunes fell. He'd survived famine and feast. Life had been a grand adventure and it had never meant more than a jolly run, he a casual observer.

Now, things were different and he realized what a fool he'd been all along. Life had value and every minute was precious.

If nothing else, he owed that to Holly. She made life precious for him and if not for her, he might have died not ever knowing the truth of it all.

"Well, Immortal, what say you now?"

He pushed away from Holly and felt her pain as sharply as he did his own.

"I'm ready," he said. Straightening his spine, he lifted his chin and stared straight into the old Reaper's face. "The question is, are you?"

Renault glared at him. "I've been waiting an eternity for this moment. On your knees; accept your fate."

For the first time since meeting the ancient Mage, Max saw the vision of the creature he truly was — older than time, fearful and shrinking against his scythe. A pitiful being, really. His soul was necrotic, reeking of rot, fear, and death.

Max sank to his knees, the sound of Holly's single sob bruising his heart.

"I feel sorry for you, old Mage. A being can have all the magic in this world and the next, it still won't fill the emptiness inside of him."

That was the crux of it all. Renault was a pathetic, empty being, who somehow lost himself in his hatred and insurmountable jealousy.

Max's thoughts must have shown on his face because he watched the Reaper's expression change from furious insanity to maniacal rage.

"Are we going to do this, or what?" Max asked trying to get the Reaper to throw his magic at him.

The old beast eyed him suspiciously. "So, now you want to die?"

"Not at all. You're beginning to bore me."

He started forward, but then froze in mid step. "Give me this fool to take, Reaper Dent. Ending his life will be a pleasure."

Max watched Holly hesitate. Her eyes brimmed with

tears and he couldn't mistake the slight quiver of her chin. This was the worst thing she would ever do and he felt like a monster for making her do it.

But he had no choice.

"Trust me," he whispered to her.

With a barely noticeable nod, she took a breath. "High honor, Reaper Renault, I now give you all control over this subject..."

Max held his breath. They were down to the last of it now. He imagined it would go very fast, the Reaping. In the time of a single breath, his life would end and he would pass into the ages.

No one knew what was in the next realm, those that had already passed were not always forthcoming with information. Some thought the way you lived this life would determine your fate, others, not so much. Even ghosts were tight-lipped. After all, they'd elected to remain behind.

But, whatever lie beyond his Reaping, Max was ready to face it. This was for Holly. Not just her alone but her future. The preservation of her life, her family and friends. And to give her time to meet a man that would ultimately fulfill her dreams. Although, that thought did sting him a bit. To think of Holly with someone else...

"Get on with it, girl," Renault growled. "Say the name."

Holly shot the old man a sharp look, but when she began to speak, she turned back to Max. Her eyes tight on his, all her emotion — fury, frustration, and love — shone through and her voice trembled when she said his name. He heard it surround him, encase him in her fierce possession of him, and shore up her resolve. He sensed a part of her would perish with this act and he grieved for her.

Outside, the wind howled and tree limbs crashed as debris slammed against the side of the manse.

"Maximillian Hyland."

The very atmosphere snapped around them. The bubble of sanity popped and Max realized that Holly had been holding him in her thoughts, suspending him, protecting him in her psychic fortress.

The moment she let go, the air exploded into flames around him. He was instantly enveloped in the old Reaper's pain, fear, and gut-wrenching hatred. The depth of the master Reaper's madness added another layer of agony to his already dreadful state.

"At last," Renault declared in a triumphant tone. "You've no idea how long I've waited for this moment." He walked closer until he stood facing Max, eye to eye.

"As crazy as you are, I think I have a pretty good idea," he ground out, though the very act of speech tore at his throat. Max would not let the crazy man have the last word, though each word he uttered ripped into his throat with demonic agony.

"Please," Holly begged behind them. "End his suffering."

"Why, Reaper Dent, you really do care?" He turned toward Max. "And, how noble you are to sacrifice yourself for her. Or, is there perhaps another, more selfish reason? Want to avoid meeting with the High Council? Facing centuries of imprisonment must be terrifying for an Immortal."

Max's blood ran cold. Of course, he'd not been looking forward to that, but a thousand years of imprisonment versus death? While neither were desirable, as an Immortal, he was used to waiting.

A thousand years was a bit much, but still doable.

Death, on the other hand, was final.

Death was no 'do-overs.'

Death was an endlessly deep chasm of isolation.

So imprisonment wasn't really that bad.

Even if it meant he would never be with Holly again, at least if she had her chance at life and happiness, then it would be worth it. If there was one thing Immortals were familiar with, it was loneliness.

Then again, maybe death was preferable after all.

But Max could not let the Reaper think he'd done them any favors.

"Pah," Max scoffed. "A thousand years or twenty, it makes no difference. I've had a good run. Do your worst... if you dare."

That was when the first wave hit him.

If he'd been in pain before, it was but a pin prick to the solid wall of skin shredding torture that now ripped his flesh.

It was such horrible feeling that Max didn't realize the screaming he heard was coming from him.

To his surprise, one moment he was caught in a maelstrom of pain, and the next he found a tiny island of comfort.

"Holly?" he sought her through the white haze. "What are you doing?"

"Helping you," she told him, her voice straining against the monumental energy she expended. "I'm going to make your passing easier." She bit down a sob. "It's the least I can do."

Renault must have realized what she was doing because he roared in fury behind her. As he did, his energy output tripled and cut through the wall of protection that Holly had erected around Max.

His agony returned, but the shock and fury of it hit Max so hard, he lost all awareness of everything outside of his torture.

Max instinctively knew that the end was near. Once the

Reaper let him loose, he would be forever gone from this plane of existence. Death, and whatever mystery it held, was now nigh.

He sought out Holly one final time. Whether to say good-bye, to thank her for all that she'd given him, or tell her he loved her, Max didn't know. He knew he couldn't face what lie ahead of him without one final touch of her thoughts intertwined with his own.

Instead, he opened his eyes to see the old Reaper, arms raised, body encased in a white-hot glow.

But Holly was near-by, and at the very moment that Renault enveloped Max she raised her scythe and unleashed her power on her former mentor. Max felt the old man waver under the onslaught, but he didn't fall.

His shock turned anger and he spun to face her.

"How dare you?" He aimed his scythe at her and the full force of his power exploded from it, knocking her back so fiercely that Max was sure she'd not survive the attack.

All hope left him. Her essence winked out and Max was sure he'd lost her.

Before he could act, the world disappeared and he fell into the endless pit of nothingness, an unending void of nonexistence.

But worse than the pain he suffered, the loss of his life, and all he knew, was going into eternity with the knowledge of Holly's defeat.

Max cried out, a muted, empty sound that echoed in his soul before the velvet darkness of eternity swallowed him whole.

CHAPTER NINETEEN

RAZOR CLARITY SLICED THROUGH HOLLY as the old man's fury consumed Max. Despite Renault's superior power, she managed to keep the tiniest thread of contact with Max. Thankfully, he'd managed to salvage some scrap of himself and it was enough for her to set her anchor on.

That small contact energized her. Was it possible that she could somehow draw energy from him to add to her own and together they could defeat the old Reaper?

As soon as the thought occurred to her, Renault launched his attack.

A wall of energy hit her, knocking her twenty feet backwards, and if for her quick action of rolling into a ball and absorbing the force of the blow, she surely would have been killed.

The very second she landed on her feet, Renault snapped her thread to Max and sent her psyche reeling.

The old Reaper cackled. "Think to outsmart me, girl?"

Despite his bravado, Holly sensed a change in him. Max was right. Reaping had sapped his strength. She didn't know how long his diminished capacity would last, so she needed to act quickly.

"I mean to stop you, no matter what it takes."

"Foolish child. You can't best me. You never could and

you certainly can't now. All the empathy in the world won't change the fact that you're a low-level Reaper at best."

Suddenly, a jolt of energy wrapped around her. It was like walking into a warm kitchen after being out in the cold. She instantly absorbed the power and added it to her own.

Max may be beyond the veil, but his last act was to give her his magic. Holly felt her strength renew, her power doubling as she uttered her challenge.

"I'm sorry it has to end this way..."

Holly didn't wait for him to build his power up any more; she launched her assault. The air crackled around her as she drew in the forces of energy — water, air, earth and magnetic energy— all fell to her command. She felt the pinnacle of her life force gather, and in the next instant, she was launching it all at Renault.

Though his power was depleted and he didn't have time to plan his own attack, he was a tenacious old Reaper. He staggered back as the wave of energy hit, but instead of going down he seemed to absorb some of it. The sheen of madness returned to his eyes and he lifted his arms once again, scythe glowing white-hot in his grasp.

He screamed in a high-pitched frenzied wail. "It's time I send you into the abyss with your lover."

He turned the tide of the battle upon her, striking at her again and again, pummeling her with all his power.

Fortunately, Holly could fend off the blows, but doing so severely limited her ability to shore up her energy for a major strike.

It was true. He had superior power and centuries worth of experience how to wield it. She would have to out-maneuver him or run the risk of him beating her down until fatigue took over and she could no longer fight him. She knew if she let off at all, it would give him time to rebuild his energies.

Near panic from the thought of losing to him, she wracked her brain to find a weakness, one thing that would make it possible to best him.

"What's the matter, girl? Not strong enough? Your magic inadequate to the task? Relinquish your magic to me and I'll give you an easy death..."

It was near impossible to concentrate with his unrelenting attacks and maddening taunts...

That's when it happened. Whether by instinct or another magical force, Holly knew how to defeat him. She could have kicked herself for not realizing it sooner.

Though it was a struggle, Holly started to ease back her assault, bit by bit, still hitting him, but with less and less force.

"Feeling tired, are we?" he asked, laughing at her show of weakness.

"I'll fight you until my last breath," she told him, playing into his delusion. "You'll have to kill me to win. Can you do that, Master Renault? Can you kill another Reaper? One who was your student and your friend?"

His laughter returned, high pitched and maniacal, a brittle, unnerving sound. "Of course. You've always been a disappointment, you know. Your tender heart, your weeping emotional sludge. All the time you were sympathizing with those wretched souls, it only drained you of your life's energies. It made you weak and malleable. If you hadn't taken a fancy to the Immortal, why I daresay a flea could have bested you with no effort at all."

It galled her to think of the Reaper's vitriol. "So, the reason you've lived so long and become so powerful wasn't because of your superior powers at all, but because somewhere down the ages you lost your heart. Instead,

you protected your own worthless soul in exchange for
their pain."

In the end, there was one part small of himself that
Renault had preserved, one small part of his psyche that
remained whole and unprotected, leaving him vulnerable.

His pride.

And as everyone knew, pride goeth before the fall.

Renault was about to plummet into a hole the size of
his own ego — and it would be deeper than the Grand
Canyon.

And Holly was going to push him over the edge.

Though he'd been left to guard the front of the manse,
Cravens knew the moment his master began to fail. The
house shook with the energy blasts exploding within.
Dust rose from around the manse and the stone structure
groaned with every hit.

"Master," he said, turning to abandon his post at the end
of the drive.

"Not so fast, buttface," a woman said behind him.

Spinning around, he saw an ebony-haired Amazon
woman standing at the end of the walk. Her copper hair
was pulled back and spun into a thick braid that went
down to her calves. She had wide eyes the color of jade
and moved like a giant tiger, every step smooth and calcu-
lated. It was clear that the woman clearly had a deadly edge
to her. And, she wasn't alone. She held a blond haired, fair
skinned unconscious man upright, his arm draped over
her shoulders. He stood only because of her support.

"You are trespassing," he told her. "You need to leave
and take that pathetic wretch with you."

"Oh, really?" Her eyes narrowed and her face reddened
to the color of charred rust. "I don't think so. This wretch
is my boyfriend, and he isn't pathetic. He's dying and your

master is the one responsible for his pending demise. I mean to end that selfish lowlife, and if you get in my way, I'll be sending you back to the slimy, hellish pit from which you emerged."

"I doubt that," Craven said. Then, without hesitation, he drew his blade and lunged.

Dropping her charge, she easily twisted out of the path of his sword. Spinning around, she lunged sideways and sent a vicious kick that missed his midsection by mere millimeters

The woman was fast; he'd give her that. But he was determined. A seasoned fighter, he'd crossed blades with many, whether a battle axe or a fencing sword, he was an expert in the field of swordsmanship.

"Foolish creature," the woman said, running toward him, ducking and dodging his every strike. "I am Fiona of the Stryker Clan. You can't best me, Shinigami. Lay down your weapons now or risk facing a Reaper yourself."

Craven ignored her threat. "No chance of that, wolf girl. I've been bending the iron since before your grandfather was whelped. Turn and run now. Take that rotting carcass with you and I might let you live."

The woman spoke no more but charged him full on, literally running into his blade. So, he struck her, again and again. But, every time the metal cut into her, it was no deeper than a paper cut and disappeared almost immediately.

"I can see your expertise, devil. Tell me, what were your other opponents made of? Tin foil? Tissue paper?" She laughed and came close enough to raise her fist. As she did so, he saw her change, her body shifting into full on wolf-woman. She was at least a foot and a half taller, her slender figure now ripped with muscles, and both her hands morphed into thick, sharp claws.

"Blasted woman," he cursed. "Get away from me."

Even as he shouted, she landed a blow square on his jaw. It was so powerful he heard the bones of his face crack. Not only that, but his body went suddenly limp and he realized she must have broken his neck as well. His vision swam and he felt his body hit the ground with a thud. He even heard the clatter of his blade against the walkway.

"You've killed me," he choked.

"It's called a paralyzing blow. Stay down and you might yet live. It's only a stunner, but if you push yourself too soon, it'll be snap goes the beastie."

The next thing he knew, she turned and retrieved her near-corpse boyfriend. Dragging the body with her, she stepped over him and marched right out of his field of vision. Unable to do anything, he listened while she made the way into the manse until he heard the door creak and then slam shut.

It didn't matter that she'd spared his life. Once his master learned that Cravens had failed, he'd be sent on the Reaper's journey at the earliest opportunity.

CHAPTER TWENTY

HOLLY KNEW THE MOMENT HER victory was eminent. Renault was so intent on ending her, that he drained his strength to the point where his attacks were little more than a flash of light, rather than true psychic energy.

"I beg you, Master Renault, please stop. For your own sake, end this and let the fates take pity on you."

He laughed again, a light, babbling sound and she knew his psyche was now as fragile as a bubble about to pop. "Worried are you, girl? You should be. I'm about to finish you. Any second now..."

Holly could stand no more. The time had come to end the charade and do as she'd promised Max. She had to put down her former mentor once and for all. Despite him Reaping Max and all of those he sent to their demise without even the slightest touch of empathy, she still took no joy in his ending.

No longer a megalomaniacal killer, he was nothing more than a sad, demented creature, victim of his own grand delusions.

She was grateful that while he'd thought it a weakness, Holly had felt the loss of every person she'd ever Reaped.

It was the deep course of her emotions that had given her the ultimate strength.

But loving the Immortal was an entirely different thing.

It was Max's love that made finding her own strength possible, after all. Love, like grief and empathy, was not a weak emotion. When used for good, they far over powered the negative emotions.

Love always reigned over hate.

"This is for you, Max," she said, just before unleashing her power. "I'm sorry, Master Renault. I know you won't be able to forgive me but I've no choice. I know you won't believe it, but I'm doing this so you can find your peace."

Holly met her mentor with her chin up and eyes forward. Drawing a breath, she concentrated on gathering all the energy that she'd buried deep within her soul. Like a summer squall, she drew the power back and then unleashed the electrical current of magic, it's tendrils spreading out like an opening fist.

"You can't beat me," he cried out in rage. "I'm invincible."

He lifted his arms to strike out at her, but the last of his magic had left him. He would never be a threat again, but would likely never regain his sanity, either.

"I believe it was the grief of Reaping that caused your madness, so I'm going to make this as easy on you as possible. I beg you, don't fight it."

Renault raised his fists and roared. "I will oppose you to the end. Surrender to my superiority!"

"End him, Holly. He doesn't deserve to keep breathing after what he's done."

Holly spun around and saw Fiona standing in the doorway. She was holding Matty, barely keeping him upright.

"I'm so sorry," Holly said. The ache of losing Max cutting her deep. "I wish we could have figured out another way."

"Another way? You say that like you had a choice."

"In the end, it wasn't my choice that mattered. It was Max's. He made it possible for me to vanquish Renault once and for all."

Fiona's ire evaporated. She leaned sideways and saw the mumbling old Reaper pacing behind Holly. "Oh, well, I suppose you should get on with it then."

"Thank you," Holly said, as the woman eased her boyfriend to the ground. Then, kneeling, she slipped to the floor, and cradled his head in her lap.

"Ah, my sweet laddie. You were a rose indeed. Of course, ye were a prickly one, to be sure."

Wanting to give the woman privacy, Holly turned back to her former mentor. He'd diminished even more in the last few moments.

"Go to your peace, Georges Renault. You've fought the hard fight. Time to let eternity have its way."

"Yes," he muttered. "I will rule eternity..."

Holly took a deep breath, and focused, drawing up from the depth her magic. In full Reaper mode, she reached out to him.

In the end, it had been no easy thing, Reaping the former master. He fought her, meeting each touch of her powers with a struggle of his own. Knocking her back again and again until it took every bit of her strength to finally get him in position.

"Don't do this, Holly. I'm begging you," he mewled at the end. "I only did as I was compelled to do, you know. You would have done the same."

"You're wrong," Holly said, but there was nothing but sadness in her tone. "It was all too much for you. Death, any death is a loss. By not acknowledging your grief you merely caused it to corrode your soul until the pathways to your humanity were lost."

"No. You're wrong. You don't know what's right. They council is a failure and all of creation is getting out of hand. They need to be put down." He looked up at her, wrapping his arms around his waist, rocking. "I know what you want. So be it. Come rule with me. Together we can... We can..."

His end was near. A slow, gentle ebb and flow into the next realm. It was both a diminishing and a healing. It was her hope that at last, his soul would be restored once he stood on the other side.

"Go in peace, old one. Calm the waters of your soul," she chanted the old words over him.

Then, at the very last of it, when he was no more than a shadow, he finally settled. "You are a good Reaper, Holly Dent. My finest achievement by far..."

Then, like the gentle pop of a soap bubble, he was gone and Holly remained.

What had to be done was finished. Master Renault was gone.

And with him, the last remnants of the insane course of events that had changed her forever. She did the job, but it was Max and his brother who'd paid the price.

And, once again, Holly was alone.

Truly, utterly, alone.

Taking a breath, Holly finally let her emotions loose, hot tears swelled forth and her chest heaved as she sobbed. It was her time to grieve and she didn't turn away from it. She opened her heart and gave herself to it.

She was so caught up in her emotions that she almost missed the room changing around her. From the dim recesses of the ancient mansion, she was transported to another place. A place of light, of life and death, a place of endings and beginnings.

She didn't know how long the process took, but when

she opened her eyes again she was awash in glaring fluorescence. She'd been taken to a warm, inviting place, as though she were standing in a field of daisies, bathed in warm sunlight.

"Hello," a familiar voice greeted here. "Fancy meeting you here."

"What the...?"

Jumping to her feet, Holly spun around, searching the bright recesses of her new location to find the last person she'd ever expected to see.

Max didn't know how much time had passed when existence began to gather around him once again. Like the sun rising over a quiet sea, there was no glorious arrival awaiting him. No separating of the clouds or burst of heavenly light to reveal morning, but rather a slow, lessening of the darkness. It wasn't long before the world came into being around him.

"What the devil?" he muttered, his throat dry and his voice coarse and uneven.

He heard several voices at once and it took a few minutes for the sound to morph into words rather than garbled speech.

"The devil has nothing to do with it, sir."

"How could he even insinuate such a thing," another voice said.

"Extremely rude, if you ask me," said yet another.

"Please," Max called out. "I apologize if I've offended you, um, whoever you are."

After a few more seconds passed, his vision returned. Blinking, he saw them at last. Three beings, more light than form, stood over him. It was hard to tell what sort of beings they were, but as his senses sharpened, it was easy to see that they were two males and one female.

"There he is," one of the men said. "Come back among the living, have we?"

Max shook his head. "Is that what this is?"

The woman coughed. "In a way. Well, not really."

"Where am I, exactly?"

"This is the chamber of the First Guild of Reapers," the woman said.

Max let out a breath he hadn't realized he'd been holding. The brief hope that stirred within him suddenly dissipated. "Right. We're back to this, are we? My trial will commence. A thousand years of prison, yadda, yadda, yadda..."

The three looked back and forth between them. Obviously, something wasn't right.

"About that," the woman began. "We have made a decision regarding your fate. Granted it was rushed, but given what's already transpired, we thought it best to make the decision and declare your sentence."

"Right."

He'd had a small hope the he somehow survived his ordeal, that he'd been given the chance to go back to Holly and lead a happy life. His heart sank at the thought he might never see her again.

"Maximillian Hyland, Immortal of the First order, we now pronounce your sentence..."

Max sat unmoving, stunned after hearing the High Council's decree. Their words still rang in his ears and for all the hoping and pleading he'd done since this bizarre ordeal began, in the end, it would make no difference in the outcome.

No difference at all.

"Max?" She hardly breathed. Was it possible? Had he survived?

Or had something even worse transpired? Was it her turn to descend into Renault's madness?

Had she died and passed into the eternal realm?

Never mind, she scolded herself. *Stop trying to figure out the universe.*

Max was with her and that was all that mattered.

Suddenly, he was there and pulling her into his arms, wrapping his body around hers. She was suddenly enveloped by a firm, warm wall of man, banishing the chill that had settled in her.

"Ah, woman, you feel so darn good."

She felt his chest move as he exhaled.

She felt his heart beat against her cheek.

She felt his love touch every fiber of her being.

"Max. You're alive." Her tears flowed again, this time out of joy instead of grief. "How is it possible?"

He pulled back and held her at arm's length.

"Silly woman. I told you I only have one magical power." He grinned, pulling her back into his embrace. "I don't die."

"What?"

He tapped his chest. "Immortal. I guess you're going to be stuck with me."

"I guess I am," Holly said, reaching behind his neck and pulling him down. "It could be worse. Immortals are stubborn, self-centered, foolish beings. But, on the other hand, they are kind, considerate, and capable of great courage."

He smiled. "And I think you're pretty neat, too. Come here."

The next thing she knew, Max was kissing her. And, not one of those friendly, light tap on the lips, grandma kisses, either.

A full mouth, tongue tangling, soon-to-be lovers type of kiss. One where promises were made and souls were surrendered.

A kiss that in one single act, brought two people together and set them on the road to a long, fulfilled life together.

"Um, excuse us," the woman said behind them.

The shock of another's presence wrenched Max from her arms, and for some reason, Holly was caught between the shock of being discovered and anger at being disturbed.

"Yes?" Max said, still gazing into Holly's eyes. "What is it now?"

The woman council member cleared her throat. "Mistress Dent, and Master Hyland, there is the matter of your future that needs to be discussed."

"Future? What is she talking about?" Holly pulled back from Max. "Oh, no. They're taking you, aren't they? The trial is over and you've been sentenced? Already? How long have they given you?"

He cast his eyes downward before speaking again. "I'm sorry, Holly. It's worse than we thought. I've been sentenced to life."

She stepped back, stunned by the news. The shock of him being taken from her once and for all was too much to bear. Her knees went out and the next thing she knew, she was falling to the floor, the room turning gray around her.

"Wait," she heard him call out. "Don't you dare pass out on me."

Somehow, his words gave her strength and the world started to settle around her.

"I'm sorry," she muttered.

He laughed, a full throated and joyous sound. "It's not you who should apologize, I'm the one who's sorry."

"That's very noble of you, but you're the one who got life."

"Sweet Holly," he said, kissing her lightly, this time. "The life I was sentenced to was with you. If you'll have me, that is."

Holly's heart thudded wildly in her chest and her throat went suddenly dry. "With me?" she croaked. "They're going to let us stay together?"

"They are, indeed. What luck, eh?"

"I don't understand...?"

The councilwoman stepped forward as Max pulled Holly to her feet once again. "Reaper Dent, our decision has been made in evidence of the supreme sacrifice Master Hyland was willing to make, to put down the threat that Master — that is — *late* Master Renault sought to perpetrate upon us all. Any judgments pending against Mr. Hyland have been permanently absolved and he is restored to his full status as an Immortal."

Max hugged Holly even tighter. "You see? Great news, huh? It fairly knocked me off my feet when they told me, you know."

"I don't doubt it." She sighed. Then, another thought occurred to her. "Um what about Mr. Hyland's brother? He died when Max was taken."

"Oh." Max sagged against her.

The councilwoman held up her hand. "His life is fully restored as well. He had no involvement in any of this and we certainly don't want to face more legal entanglements"

"A wise choice," Max said, clearly relieved.

"Then, let's go home," Holly said. She was anxious to get back to the funeral home, back to a soft bed, a hot meal, and a cold beer.

"Of course, Mistress Dent," the tall man said. "There is one more thing. Have you thought about what you will do now?"

Holly looked up at Max. "I want nothing more than to be with Max. Which means I'm afraid I'm resigning my position. Sorry to quit without notice, but I don't think I can ever do another Reaping after all that's happened."

"It is understandable that you'd feel that way. But the guild needs your talents. Please take your time and reconsider. We had hopes you would remain, perhaps in a different capacity."

"Different capacity? Of what sort?" Max asked.

"Wait." Holly held up her hand. "I don't think..."

"You should hear her out," Max told her. "They seem somewhat desperate."

Holly looked at the Council. "Okay. I'll bite. What job would I be doing?"

"We recently had to remove one of our council members from his service and we have an opening. Please consider serving with us. Your expertise and empathy for your clients are exactly what we need."

"It's true," the first councilman said. "We've become rather stale, without a clear vision. Perhaps what happened was our fault, or at least partly so. We've become so closed off from the living that we'd forgotten what our subjects were experiencing. In all the time that you've been with us, you've never forgotten that the most important part of our job is the soul given to our care. You would be doing us a great service."

Holly didn't know what to think. She looked to Max who shrugged his shoulders.

"Whatever makes you happy is fine with me. Really."

"I need some time before I give you an answer."

"Take as long as you need, my dear," the councilwoman said. "After all, nothing around here moves forward overnight. I believe the term 'snail's pace' was first used when speaking about our guild."

To Holly's surprise, the two council members started making a most unpleasant sound, a mixture between chirping and screeching. It took a few moments to realize that they were actually laughing.

"Very well, then. I'll be in contact."

In the next instant, she and Max were sent back to the crumbling manse and the two people who waited there for them.

CHAPTER TWENTY-ONE

IT HAD BEEN ONE HECK of a long day. Max put out a bottle of Merlot and prepared them a light meal of exotic cheeses, fresh sliced vegetables, tropical fruit, cold cuts, and freshly-baked baguettes.

"Looks wonderful," Holly yawned as she walked into the living room. "I'm starving."

Max grinned. "It's not the lavish meal I'd hoped to prepare but since Millie has gone for the evening and I didn't feel like another trip to the all-night diner. This was my best solution."

"Wine, meat, cheese, fruit, veggies and fresh bread? A veritable feast."

"Then let's dig in."

"I thought you'd never ask."

Thirty minutes later, the food was consumed, the fire burned warmly in the fireplace, and for the first time in his extensive memory, Max felt complete.

"This is nice," Holly said beside him.

Snuggled together on the overstuffed sofa, they watched the fire slowly die down until it was nothing but glowing embers.

Max leaned forward and emptied the remainder of the wine into their glasses. "Want another bottle?"

"Not right now. Let's just sit and do nothing for a while."

"Deal," he said. "It's so nice, being here with you. I mean, I've been with women before..."

"Oh, gosh, you're not going to tell me all about your dating life, are you? Because, I think that's conversation we need to put off for another time. Or, never, would be good."

He laughed. "Nothing like that. What I was going to say is that I just realized I've never felt completely comfortable with a woman before."

"Really? Why not?"

He shrugged. "I think it's because I was either trying to please them or trying to disengage from them. But never really trying to know them."

"I think the operative word here is 'trying.'"

Max sat back. "What do you mean?"

"Well, if you feel about me the way I feel about you, there's no trying. It doesn't have a switch you can turn on and off, but rather it just is. This thing exists and it's from both of us."

He thought about it a moment. "What does your friend Artemis think about all that's happened?"

Holly laughed. "Yeah, she was like 'what took you so long?' She's been pulling for you since the beginning, believe it or not." She sipped her wine. "What about your friends and family? Do you think there'll be any objections?"

"I don't think I care one way or the other, to tell the truth. Matty will be his usual annoying self, probably telling you that you can do better. Fiona will be thrilled, of course. And Melody and the rest of the staff have already intimated that they'd be thrilled if we, um, 'got together,' so to speak."

She sighed and settled back into his arms. "I'm glad. After everything we've been through, I'd do it all again it if it meant us being together."

"Me, too." It was his turn to sigh. "You came to Reap me and got way more than you bargained for."

Holly grinned. "In other words, I pursued me until you caught me."

They laughed together and Max knew that the compass he'd been missing had finally appeared and he couldn't wait to start their life together.

It was with that thought that he slid off the sofa to land kneeling on the floor in front of her.

"Holly Elizabeth Dent," he began. "Would you do me the honor of becoming my wife?"

She sat there, mouth open staring at him, her face frozen in shocked surprise.

For a moment, Max was sure she was going to turn him down. He was just about to pull away from her when she spoke.

"I will marry you and be your wife until my very last breath."

He grinned. "And I will love and cherish you for just as long."

Moving back up to sit beside her, he took Holly in his arms and kissed her long and deep. The beautiful Reaper who'd come to take his soul had given him his life instead. When it came time for him to pass into the ages, he would go a happy man who'd gotten the greatest gift of all.

A woman who loved him.

❧

Holly sat on Max's sofa, his arms around her, nestled in his embrace and covered by a thick quilt. The fire had long since died out, and she could see the hint of dawn slowly lighting the early morning sky.

They'd talked well into the night until Max finally gave in to his exhaustion, the food, and the wine. She wasn't far behind him and suspected that they'd spend the day like this, wrapped in each other's arms.

Just then, Artemis glided into the room and made her perch on the fireplace mantle. "I take it you won't be coming upstairs, any time soon?"

"Oh gosh. I forgot to put out your seed," Holly said, suddenly feeling guilty at ignoring her friend. "There's some bits of mango left out in the kitchen, if you don't mind helping yourself."

"Already did. Fortunately, I was able to bump the spigot enough to get water, too. Though, you might want to shut if off."

"I'm sorry you had to fend for yourself."

"You've been through a lot, so you're forgiven. Um, this time, anyway."

"Thank you," Holly yawned.

The bird ruffled her feathers. "Guess I'll head back upstairs and give you some privacy."

"You don't have to go. I'm going to pass out in a few minutes and I have a feeling that Max won't be budging for hours. Please stay."

"Very well." She settled into a large glass candy dish. "Things are good, then?"

Holly grinned. "Oh, better than good. He asked me to marry him tonight."

"You better have accepted." The bird leaned forward.

"Don't worry, I did."

"Good."

A few quiet moments passed between them. Holly envisioned life with Max. Staying up late and rising early. Going on long walks together. Eating at all the amazing restaurants in Nocturne Falls. Telling their families and friends. Maybe one day raising children together...

"Hey, Cinderella," Artemis said. "One quick question."

"What's that?"

"What's it going to be? Indoor or outdoor?"

Holly blinked. "Indoor or outdoor, what?"

The bird started to cackle. "Wedding, silly. Indoors or outdoors? Under the gazebo at the park, or in a rented hall? Spring wedding or fall commitment ceremony? Come on, girl, have you never even attended a wedding?"

Holly sat back, her stomach tightening and her head swimming with a sudden burst of thoughts, each more dire than the one before it. Jumping to her feet, she began to pace.

Her movements, though not all that loud, were enough to rouse Max.

"Holly? What is it?" he asked, rubbing his eyes. "Something wrong? Did the council change its mind?"

Holly shook her head. "No. It's far worse than that, I'm afraid."

"What's wrong?"

She rushed back into his arms, trembling as he held her. But, she didn't flee as was her first inclination. No, best to handle it face on.

"What's wrong is us. We have a wedding to plan, a venue to choose. Dresses. Bridesmaids and groomsmen. Cake for the reception. Oh, gosh, we have to plan a reception..."

He quickly pulled her into his embrace. "Hey, hey, hey. You forget who you're with. A wedding is nothing but a big party. I plan parties all the time."

"You plan funerals."

"Well, they're not always sad. I mean, if their family's not especially fond of them, that is."

That was when Holly's panic bubble burst. "How absurd I am, only hours since we both came close to losing each other for all eternity, to carry on about something so silly."

"Not silly at all," he said but she could tell he wasn't a

hundred percent on that. The fact that he was trying to calm her fears made him all the more adorable.

"I guess everything hit me all at once. Please, forgive me."

He pulled her back into his arms. "There's nothing to forgive, Reaper girl. We've faced down life and death. Planning a wedding will be easy peasy. I promise."

"Of course, it will. Besides, we don't have to do this, you know."

He looked down at her. "Get married, you mean?"

It was her turn to laugh. "Oh, no. You're totally committed to that. We don't have to have a wedding. We can elope."

"But that would be disappointing our friends and families. I don't know about you but facing down a maniacal evil Reaper is a lot less frightening."

"Right." She laughed. "Whatever we do, we're in this together, eh?"

"Yes, we are. Like it or not, you and I are going to be married a very, very long time."

"Forever, right?"

He sealed his promise with another kiss and Holly reveled in the thought that while she'd once been set on Reaping the Immortal, he'd given her so much more. And there was so much more ahead of them.

ABOUT PAM

SINCE THE AGE OF 13, Pamela Labud wanted to be a writer. So much so, that she asked her Mom and Dad for a typewriter for Christmas that year. Now, a multi-published author, whose first book was a 2006 Double RITA finalist, she has finally realized that dream.

In addition to writing Paranormal, Contemporary, and Historical she also writes Medical romance novels. A Registered Nurse, Pamela worked 34 years in ICU and Cardiac Care. Married, she shares her home with 6 dogs, 3 Cockatiels, 2 Love Birds, 4 Parakeets, and 3 Zebra Finches.

When she's not writing, Pam enjoys watching TV crime shows, old movies and anime, reading romance fiction, suspense and Manga.

You can check out Pamela's books at;
www.pamlabud.com.

Printed in Great Britain
by Amazon